Lunen

BOOK 1: TRIBLOOD

BY AHMED AL-SHEIKH

ISBN: 978-0-692-79541-5

DEDICATION

To My Family and Friends for all the Love and Support.

TABLE OF CONTENTS

CHAPTER 1:
The Fated Meeting

You can do this, I know it. The words kept running through her mind. But Winifred Winters always seemed to harbor doubt. To make matters worse, this was not the simple doubt of wondering whether she'd left the lights on at home. This was the doubt that gnaws at the spirit, forcing you to shortchange everything about yourself, regardless of how talented or well-liked you actually are. She always felt this way when she had to speak with her father.

"Just dial the number, Win," Jennifer Pike whispered in her best reassuring voice. How Winifred got such a roommate was beyond her. The contrasts were too great. Jennifer wore her blonde hair in a pixie cut straight from a magazine, her shimmering emerald eyes gazing back over a supermodel smile. Winifred brushed her shoulder-length, wavy auburn hair out of the way of glasses that made her blue eyes appear simple and unimpressive. She had only recently gotten rid of her braces, at the age of twenty-two, leaving her with only a shy, quiet smile. Jennifer always spoke her mind and managed to achieve her goals, both in and out of the classroom at their college. Winifred never spoke up, even when it came to what nickname she would rather have, which was simply Winnie. Now, she struggled to find the nerve to talk to her father about her slipping grades.

Dr. Stephen Winters was an accomplished physician and surgeon. His colleagues often spoke of him as the most likely man to cure cancer. He had a will of iron, and what he said usually was law in his family. If Winifred wanted to change her concentration in college, she would have to clear it with him. But that would probably end badly.

Her older sister, Catherine, had initially been her father's golden child because she wanted to become a surgeon too. A brilliant girl, she had managed to make it to med school with their father paying the way. In her third year, Catherine met Joseph. They fell in love and got engaged. Then she got pregnant. Dr. Winters demanded that she get an abortion so as not to be forced out of school. Catherine refused, stating that she could just go back after having the baby. He cut off the money and effectively disowned his prodigal daughter simply because she had challenged his rule.

At age five, Winifred lost her mother to leukemia. She often thought her father would not have had such demanding expectations of his children if their mother were still alive. *Well, life is never perfect.* That was her mantra for every disappointment and failed dream. And despite Jennifer's reassuring words, she was sure this phone call would be no different.

"Dad?" she asked tentatively.

"Hello, Winifred. I trust your studies are going well," replied the deep voice that both symbolized love and fear for her.

"Not exactly, Dad."

The next five minutes went exactly how she had imagined: She explained how the classes she needed to qualify for med school were not just hard but impossible for her, and as she tried to make him understand that if she did not change her major to something she was good at she would end up failing, she broke down into quiet tears. That even, cold voice stated that he was the one paying for her education, and that he would only pay for one that would be useful, not one of her strange hobbies like English literature or world history. He then said that he would talk to the dean about giving her another semester to shape up and disconnected the call.

Well, life is never perfect. And in her eyes, it seemed unlikely that it ever would be. Perhaps life was as some philosophers thought: Only a few are ever meant to rise up and be happy and successful. Everyone else is just there to support them on the way up.

Winifred was careful to be quiet as she packed her suitcase. If Jennifer caught her, she might stop and reconsider. But this had to be the only way. She left her dorm five minutes before one in the morning, dressed in her jeans and a black-and-grey striped shirt and black hooded sweater. Knowing she would have a long way to walk, she wore her sneakers.

Her plan was simple, if not a little cowardly. She would just leave. She had her sister's new address from a postcard at Christmas. After dropping out, Catherine had married Joseph and they were raising their new child. Despite everything, her sister kept on surviving. Since she was not as strong as Catherine or Jennifer, all Winifred could do was run away from her problems. By dropping out she might make her father feel something, even if it was only anger at being embarrassed by two "failure" daughters.

As she crossed the quad, it began to rain. Within moments large drops had doused everything in the vicinity, including Winifred. Her tears slowly mixed with the rain.

What is the point of life? she thought. *If there actually is a way to live when life is so unfair, I'd like to know what it is.*

Suddenly, the ground seemed to spin as a sense of vertigo washed over her. It was as if the rain had baptized her, changing how she perceived reality. She felt like she had been shot from a cannon at an unbelievable speed. Within seconds, the vertigo had vanished—and so had the ground. Against all logic, Winifred had somehow been moved ten feet into the air over a clearing in the middle of a forest. Several people in strange clothing ran below her, and she began to wonder if she was dreaming. Then gravity took effect again.

Before she crashed into the ground, one of the runners performed a leaping tackle into her, gripping her. When she did land, this stranger cushioned her body. As she looked up, all she could see before he rolled her off him and began running again were his eyes. They were the color of dark wood, as if filled with some kind of rich chocolate. And the look within them was one of such intensity, somewhere between determined and insane.

The stranger kept running with increasing, unbelievable speed and then leapt up a distance of nearly fifteen feet to a rope ladder. Winifred's eyes trailed upward, and she was startled to see a strange ship of some sort. It was as if Leonardo da Vinci had redesigned a Spanish galleon for flight, with several wing-like sails sticking out along its sides. Near the top of the various masts, propellers spun at a fantastic speed while smaller support propellers extended from the sides of the vessel. And shining from behind this ship, a full, golden moon hung in the sky.

"Hold it right there!" she heard from behind her. She turned to see men with grey-green armor covering their torsos pointing spears at her, their eyes glaring at her from behind the visors of their helmets. Winifred found the single, protruding curved horn jutting from each helm's forehead reminiscent of a rhino.

What the hell is going on? her mind screamed as they surrounded her.

"Did you feel that?"

Aboard the flying ship, two figures watched the scene of the young woman being dragged away. The taller male had asked the question in his simple voice, neither deep nor high.

The shorter female turned to look at him. "You know I'm not as perceptive to weird things as you are."

"Still, just before that girl showed up, I felt something, and…"

"And?"

"I have to go after her."

"I thought you would say that. May I ask why?"

"Something about her seems to scream out that she needs help."

"Well, obviously…"

"More than just a simple rescue," the male replied as he grabbed a cloak.

"Fine. Let me just get them to lower the ship so you can…" She stopped midsentence. He was gone. "I hope you know what you're doing," she said aloud.

I've lost my mind. That was the only logical conclusion Winifred could reach about her present situation. She stood tied to a tree, her arms bound above her head and her legs to the trunk, while a horde of men, who looked as if they had escaped from a medieval movie, screamed questions at her after ransacking her suitcase. Things like, "Where is the *Freewind* going?" and, "What moon are you from?" none of which made any sense to her in the least. She had her own questions, such as why the moon was bright yellow or where a boat that should not exist had come from.

"For the last time, I don't know what you're talking about!" she screamed.

"Don' play cute with us, girlie," one of the men said with a slight leer in his helmeted eyes. "If ya want, we could make ya more comfortable…" With that, he began to reach for her chest.

Oh my God! What is going on? Nothing makes sense. Why is this happening? I don't want this; I don't want this; I don't want this…

"Let go of me, you goddamn bastards!" she screamed.

"I agree with her," a new voice said.

The armored men turned to face the newcomer, giving Winifred enough room to see. She saw a man of average build standing at about five foot nine with a cloak wrapped around his torso like a child's security blanket. He wore his jet-black hair in a self-cut style, slowly growing out in rough bangs over his forehead. His head was round; his face and nose had no angular features. In fact, nothing about him seemed remarkable other than his eyes: a rich brown with a quiet intensity.

He came back for me? As soon as that thought entered her mind, she saw him draw a curved dagger almost a foot in length. He juggled it a few times as if it were a ball, his eyes sweeping back and forth among the men. Winifred quickly realized that even though they outnumbered him fifteen to one, none of her captors moved. In hushed voices, she heard them say something about a *Triblood.* Then the newcomer threw his dagger at her.

She screamed until she heard the blade impale the tree with a loud *thunk*; then she felt her arms fall back to her sides. She looked up to see that he had cut the rope, just a few inches away from her wrist.

"Cut yourself free, and don't lose that dagger!" he yelled before tossing the cloak at the closest man. The armored goon struggled to pull the cloth off his face, but when he did, he saw the newcomer's ebony boot just before it struck his chin, sending him crashing into a tree. Her rescuer wore white cloth pants with a black tunic and a red sash tied around his waist. By his right hip, Winifred saw a sheath for the dagger that she now held in her hands.

By now, the rest of her captors had mobilized, grabbing their spears. They surrounded him in a circle, each taking a turn trying to stab him. He quickly ducked an attack aimed at his face, rolling on the ground before leaping up and bringing his elbow into an opponent's helmeted face with a satisfying *clang*. He grabbed another's spear as it was about to dig into his chest, kicking the feet out from under his attacker. He then spun around and smashed the spear over the head of the warrior behind him. As another charged him, he swiftly reached out and gripped the horn on his attacker's helmet and twisted around, flinging the man into a tree trunk.

Winifred noticed that the way he fought was not like in martial arts films or televised competitions. There was no true pattern or art to it, just a simple, primal knowledge of how to fight. It was, for lack of a better term, raw combat.

When there were only four left, he turned to her and yelled, "Are you going to move or not?" Just then, one spearman impaled him in the stomach. A moment of silence followed. Winifred was unsure what to feel for this strange man who had come for her, when she noticed that the spearman could not draw his weapon from the wound. Her eyes flew to the stranger's face, where she saw a strange smile.

He grabbed the shaft of the spear with his left hand and brought his right fist down in a heel-palm strike, breaking it so that only a small piece of wood remained connected to the steel blade in his body. He pulled the broken shaft and its unwilling owner toward him and punched the spearman in the nose. He then pivoted on his heel and struck a backhanded fist at the man trying to take him from behind, actually smashing the faceguard off of his helmet.

Before Winifred could react, her rescuer had leapt toward her, wrapping his left arm around her, and took off running. Before she lost sight of the only three conscious men in armor, she saw the stranger swing his right hand in their direction. It felt as if he launched a gust of wind at her former captors. She was fairly certain one spearman went flying into the branches of the tree his comrade was thrown into before the rest of the woods obscured her sight.

"When someone gives you a dagger to cut yourself free, it doesn't mean 'Stand still and see what happens,' you idiot!" he yelled at her.

They had stopped running and taken shelter inside a small cave. Winifred had watched as her rescuer pulled the spearhead from his abdomen and then refused to bandage it. He simply covered it with his hand, took several deep breaths, and then began to yell at her.

"Listen, I'm grateful and all, but I'm a little freaked out by this whole thing!" she yelled back.

He gave her an appraising look before he smiled. "Fine. I'm sorry I yelled at you. I am angrier at myself for getting stabbed." He sighed. "Leave it to an idiot like me to look away during a fight."

"Well, I may be no expert on fighting," Winifred said with a slight smile, "but you did pretty good back there."

"Thanks. What do you like to be called?" he asked, taking a moment to glance below his hand at the state of the wound.

"Well, my name is Winifred Winters," she replied. She sighed. "My father calls me Winifred, and a lot of people call me Fred, and my roommate Jennifer calls me Win, but that doesn't really..." She stopped herself, realizing she'd been rambling.

"I didn't ask what people call you," the stranger said before standing up. "I asked what you like to be called."

She stared at him, dumbstruck—not because he chose to stand despite the gaping wound in his stomach that his hand somehow managed to cover but because he had actually asked her what *she* liked to be called.

"I like being called Winnie."

"Well, Winnie, it is a pleasure to meet you," he said, offering his hand to shake. "Oh, sorry. This was the one covered in blood."

"Oh my God!" she screamed. Blood still stained his tunic and a portion of his pants, and he still had blood on his stomach, but the wound had completely vanished. Not even a scar remained. "How did you do that? No one can heal like that!"

"My mother was a full Gold-mooner," he answered. When he saw the confused look in her eyes, he looked her up and down as if he was starting to see her for the first time. "I'm a Triblood. Does that not scare you?"

"I don't know what that is."

"Thought so." He sat next to her. "While I would love to explain this now, the sun is starting to rise. We should move." He took the dagger from her hand at last and then kissed the hilt before sheathing it. "For now, let's just say that I'm very strong, very fast, and heal very quickly."

"And that gust of wind from last night?" she asked, standing up at last.

"Oh, that was nothing," he said with a slight smirk in his voice as he led her out.

They had barely made it back to the clearing when the three last spearmen who were uninjured enough to actually pursue them ambushed them.

"Who *are* these guys?" Winnie asked.

"Mercenaries, most likely," the stranger replied, looking around the area. "Probably under an Imperial order to capture me and my crewmates."

"Why?"

"Piracy," he replied as though stating that the sun was out.

"*What?*" she yelled as the spearmen began to rush them.

"Technically, we're transporters for hire," he said before throwing himself at one spearman with such force and speed that they both crashed through the trees, the sounds of clashing metal and pained grunts following them. Winnie did not have time to wonder why he was so strong or fast because she took off running from the remaining two mercenaries.

She was keeping a good, quick pace, despite her own fatigue, when suddenly the ground vanished. Somehow she had run off a small ridge into a river. The river itself was only thigh-deep, but it was enough to slow her down as the spearmen leapt in after her. Still she trudged along, desperate to live.

"Winnie!"

She looked toward the direction she'd come from. There stood the man, smiling as his hand pointed above her. She gazed up to see the strange flying boat descending, its rope ladder dropping within reach. She quickly grabbed it and felt the boat pull her up.

Wait. What about him? she thought. She turned her head to see what would become of her new friend and saw what would be the first of many amazing sights for her.

He stood with his hands in front of his chest, his fingers curling as if holding a ball. He had a wild smile on his face, like a child playing a game he excelled at. His intense eyes had grown even more so with concentration. The air between his hands began to spark and ignite, and as he pulled his hands apart, a ball of fire floated over both palms.

He then brought his hands forward, sending the fire balls straight at the two mercenaries. They struggled to escape. A great crash followed as the blazing spheres exploded on impact, and, while the size of the blast was too small to kill, it was enough to send both men flying. Winnie watched as her new friend leapt from the riverbank straight at her, almost thirty feet from where he stood. He caught the ladder, slipped down one rung, and then finally gripped it tight.

Winnie stared as he smiled at her like he had just tripped coming down the stairs in front of her. Everything about him, from the fire to the wound healing and all that had occurred in between—none of it made sense. Yet he gave off such a strange feeling, like he was comfortable no matter what happened.

"Who are you?" she asked.

"Well, for starters," he replied with a smile, "I like to be called Lunen."

And that was how I met Lunen. Even if I knew what sort of journey lay ahead of me as I traveled with him, I like to think I would have still taken it. Still, as far as first encounters go, it could have been a lot better.

CHAPTER 2: Freedom within Chains

Winnie looked at the group of faces staring at her. She was unaccustomed to so much attention. In fact, the last time more than one person had paid any attention to her was when Joey Alvarez, the perpetually sick boy she knew in sixth grade, had vomited out the window, and she had been unlucky enough to be walking by. This was almost as bad.

"So who is this girl, and why did we have to delay our delivery for her?" the only other female there asked. A short girl, about a foot and a half shorter than Lunen, she had skin the color of coffee served with milk and hazel eyes that gave Winnie the harshest look she had ever been given. Her clothes resembled something from a Burt Lancaster pirate movie, and she wore a cutlass sheathed at either hip. A bandana tied off her brown, curly hair.

"Captain Liana, this is Winnie," Lunen offered with a slight smile, as though accustomed to being questioned like this. "She's something like a newmooner, so be gentle."

"Hmmmm..." one of the taller men murmured. Winnie found him strange to look at. He had the facial features of a delicate Asian woman, with the exception of short blonde hair. Yet his voice was too deep to contain a drop of estrogen. He wore a pair of half-moon spectacles in front of his dark eyes and a white coat with white pants, even white boots. "Lunen, while I am never one to bring your powers of observation into question, how, pray-tell, is she 'like a newmooner'? Either she is, or she is not."

"Ya know, Migs," a three-foot-tall man with a round body and shocking long red hair replied, "if Lunen sez this gal's something, ya know he's usually on the up 'n up. So lay off!" This man, unlike the white-clad Migs, had features more likely to appear on a hybrid of moles and monkeys than a human. His large nose seemed to hook downward. While Migs wore white, this one dressed in brown. A pair of goggles hid his eyes.

"Well, Zeg, I am sorry if I happen to notice the glaring flaws in Lunen's introduction of the young lady!" Migs snapped back.

"Ignore the twins; they bicker like this all the time," Lunen commented with a wry smile.

"They're twins?" Winnie asked in disbelief.

"Yeah. We're all still confused on that miracle," Lunen answered with less of a smile and more of a seriously-we-don't-know-how-it-happened look in his eyes.

Winnie then felt the hairs on her neck rise, and she turned quickly. Behind her stood a creature at once terrifying and beautiful: a large cat, like a black tiger. But in Winnie's mind, it couldn't be a cat because huge leather wings folded along its front legs.

"*What the hell is that?*" she screamed when she saw it.

"My sky-lynx," Lunen replied, dropping to one knee. "Did you miss me, Wind-hunter?" he cooed as he hugged its head. "Has he been a good boy while I was gone, Leito?"

"So well behaved, we knew you were all right," a huge ebony man replied in a booming bass voice from the ship's steering apparatus. Bulky with muscle, he stood seven foot eleven. What shocked Winnie most was his face; it was that of a man in his sixties, etched with scars and the wear of years of formidable experience. He had no hair on his scalp, but a long white beard hung well past his waist. He wore a chainmail shirt and black cloth pants with knee-high boots.

"Point is," Lunen called out loud enough for them all to hear, "I'm bringing her along. If she steps out of line, I'll be there to put her back." He then turned to face Liana. "She's got nowhere else to go."

Liana allowed herself a small smile before facing Winnie. "Your name again?"

"I'm Winifre…I like being called Winnie," she answered.

"I run a tight ship, Winnie," Liana said, the smile disappearing from her face. "We may be considered pirates, but we're just transporters and handymen. That is how we make our living. If you can't keep up, we make no profit."

Winnie had no idea how to respond to that, but then she felt a hand on her shoulder. She didn't have to turn to know it was Lunen.

"Trust me: this one will be able to handle it," he answered.

Winnie learned much during her first few days. She learned that the airship was called the *Freewind* and was able to fly because of a rare mineral called gaianite, an ore that gave off an energy that reacted with another strange mineral called gelix steel. The ship used the pipes made of gelix to project the energy downward, and the various propellers and oars were used to control the ship's movement in all three dimensions of height, width and length. When Zeg told her that, Winnie found it funny. She was already in a different dimension by her standards.

She also learned the various roles of the crew. Liana was obviously the captain, while the giant Leito was her first mate. The twins took care of things, Migs being the doctor and Zeg, the ship's engineer. Others were also on board, all working in some regard, be that cooking, working the huge amounts of equipment that kept the ship in the sky or working under Migs in the infirmary.

"Are there, like, a hundred people working on this boat?" she asked Lunen once.

"Two hundred seventeen and a quarter," he replied.

"How do you have a quarter?"

"Well, Wind-hunter counts as a crewmember, but he doesn't fill up the space a normal person would. And I was wrong."

"About what?"

"Now it's two hundred *eighteen* and a quarter," he answered with a smile.

The rules of the ship were simple: a person stays as long as they like, so long as they keep working. This applied both to crew and people who had no other way to pay for their transport. Lunen had the strangest series of jobs on the ship. He alternated between cleaning the ship, helping the other officers with their duties, and, oddly enough, cooking on occasion. Winnie was placed in his command, meaning she spent a lot of her time helping Lunen in his chores. She learned the hierarchy among them: Liana at the top, with Leito, Migs and Zeg answering to her as the rest of the crew answered to them.

Lunen answered to all four of them, yet he seemed separated from the rest of the crewmen. And working under him meant that Winnie had to answer to him as well as the others at the top, something that no one else on the crew did. In fact, the easiest way to tell if someone was new on the ship was to determine whether they seemed to have an issue with Lunen's presence. When she pressed those who did for a reason, she heard the same word Lunen had mentioned when they met, the same one the mercenaries seemed to be afraid to say aloud: *Triblood.*

On her first day on the ship, Winnie asked Lunen if he knew how she got to this world, and what world this even was. He only shrugged and said: "Who knows how anyone gets anywhere? And we simply call it the world. What need do we have to name it?"

As she prepared for bed on her third night sleeping on the deck with Lunen nearby, she finally built up her courage to ask him the two questions she knew she needed answers to:

"What is a Triblood, and what is the obsession with the moons?"

At that, he smiled and began to tell the story of his life.

Winnie learned that this world was a fantastic one, filled with conflict and divisions. For as long as history had been recorded there, it had always had three moons. The Red and Gold moons both hung over the same locations, their orbit following the planet's rotation. The Blue moon orbited the North Pole in an elliptical pattern, never being less than full for those who lived there.

The moons bestowed different properties on those who lived in their light. Those who lived in the deserts and mountains of the Red moon were given great physical prowess, such as speed and strength. Those in the plains and forests of the Golden moon gained great abilities of recuperation and regeneration. And those in the perpetual light of the Blue moon gained the ability to use their wills to make the elements do as they pleased.

But it was not that simple. It was not just the place of a person's birth that determined their ability. The light of the moon was also a factor. One born during a new moon would gain no enhanced abilities while those born beneath a half moon could only go so far, and those born in the light of a full moon gained what would be considered the greatest potential. The final factor lay in parentage. The light of the moon you were born under would stay with you all your life, just like the blood of your parents. Their birth-moon would be added to yours, and your birth-moon would be your gift to your child.

The hierarchy of this world was thus decided by the power of one's moons. And, as in all worlds and societies, there was prejudice.

In this world, people from the Red and Gold moons interacted often. Sometimes, children of different moon combinations were born. The Blue-mooners lived in isolation from the world, making mixed children with elemental manipulation very rare. But the rarest of all were Tribloods, who were feared and reviled everywhere. The only way a Triblood could be born was if two people left their own continents for another. Tribloods were considered the spawn of traitors and were feared for their powers. While they would never be as strong as those with three full Red-moons in their blood, or heal as fast as those with three full Gold-moons, or make the elements do things that were impossible, like the three full Blue-mooners, and thus were looked down as being less for that, Tribloods could do things with their combined abilities that made them dangerous. They were possibly the only people considered truly inhuman.

During one of the greater wars, a noblewoman of the Golden lands joined an order of healers to help soldiers on the front lines. If one had three full Gold-moons, like Azana of the house of Infinus did, they would make fantastic surgeons because they were always able to stay healthy, even in the face of plagues. During her tending of mercenary soldiers from the Red desert, she met a mighty warrior called Kabern of the tribe of Taimem. Like her, he was a full mooner, with the exception that his was red. They fell in love and were married during the conflict. As soon as they could, they made their way to the great Azure city in the North. It was there that their son was born, a child of all three moons. They named him Lunen.

Lunen lived a pleasant life at first. His father taught him methods of physical combat and defense while his mother encouraged his mind in various philosophies and arts. Lunen was privileged to learn his Blue-moon skill from the leaders of the Blue-mooners, the Five Sages, due to a debt owed to his father. The Azure city was his playground, and the Blue-mooners did not mistreat him, something the rest of the world would do if given the chance. In time, Lunen's family decided that he should see the world outside of the North. When he was ten, his trials began.

"You see," Lunen said, "we were on our way to visit my mother's family when we were boarded by the forces of a disgusting fat pig of a noble. My father patted me on the head, told me to remember that survival is often the best form of victory, and then he ran to fight. It was amazing to see. He tore into those soldiers like they were made of cheap wood. The only reason he died was because he stood his ground when a swarm of arrows flew at us. I still remember him standing tall, arrows sticking out of him, and he looked back at me and smiled. My mother and I were taken. And since I wasn't strong enough to fight them all, I made a deal."

Lohl was their captor's name. One of the more decadent lords in the Golden lands, he drew most of his wealth from the coliseum he owned. Slaves and animals fought and died there. Lohl had heard of the legendary warrior and the noblewoman who ran away to the North. When word came that they were traveling with their son, he decided he wanted that Triblood for his death matches. What he didn't expect was the child's defiant remarks.

"I'll fight in your arena for ten years. If I live that long, you let us go. Deal?"

Lohl was outraged that the child dared to speak to him in such a manner. He agreed under the added condition that the child would not see his mother for that decade, expecting that the child would die in his first match. Lunen had little choice but to accept.

"My first match was something of a nightmare. Gold-moon powers, regardless of the moon's size in your life, are at their greatest from birth. So you're always at your best for your healing. But until you both mentally and physically mature, your strength and your ability to control the elements are dependent on your concentration. As I am now, it's all instinct. But back then, I had to focus hard to fight."

Lunen's first match became the stuff of legends. A mere child of ten, he faced off against a giant full Red-mooner. His jailers thought it would be funny for the child's arms to be chained together during the match. But instead of reacting as a child would normally, he calmly stared at the clouds for a few seconds. Then he surprised everyone when he rushed across the dusty stage with a concentrated burst of speed. He had enough force in his tackle to knock his opponent off his feet.

The larger man, while still on the ground, countered with a kick that sent Lunen into the wall. Blood erupted from the child's lips as he coughed and sputtered. But to the surprise of the crowd, his opponent and his captor, he rose back up. At that moment, it began to rain hard. Lunen brought his fists above his head and then slammed them into the ground. Arcs of lightning streaked along the now-wet earth. White spider webs danced across the giant's body, and his eyes rolled to the top of his head as he fell to the ground, foaming at the mouth.

"You see, because I'm in touch with the elements, I knew it was about to rain. And I saved my strength for that moment. That, and to break the chains after I won, just so I could piss Lohl off."

For his second match, Lunen was placed in combat against an adolescent sky-lynx. A dangerous enemy because of the creatures' speed and ability to fly. To make sure they didn't escape, they were chained to the ground.

"It was so cruel what they did to him," Lunen explained. "His leg was bleeding. And even worse, his old wounds had started to heal over the manacle. So, I slowly approached him. He was on guard, but he seemed to sense I wasn't going to attack. I broke his chain and turned to leave him, and he just followed me. Since then, Wind-hunter has always been with me."

*****

For years Lunen fought in the arena, without seeing his mother. He restrained his desire to contact her, knowing that it would violate his agreement with Lohl. Lunen was a man of his word, even if it meant living with the sorrow of her being so close and yet out of reach. As he fought, the legend of the Triblood who defied Lohl grew—and so did Lohl's rage.

"You see, after a few years, my powers really kicked in, and I became a king of the arena. I started to learn how to instinctively combine my Red and Gold-mooning to survive almost anything. And if things became desperate, I could rely on my Blue-mooning. But I kept focusing on the remaining two years until my freedom was my own."

"What happened?" Winnie asked.

"Liana and the crew did."

A former adventurer from the Red desert, Liana's father was one of the strongest in the world, a mere half-moon difference keeping him from the level of power Lunen's father possessed. Ever the enterprising man, he bought an airship and started a business of transportation in his youth. However, because the Empire demanded control of all trade around the world, the crew of the *Freewind* were considered pirates. When they were finally captured, they were forced into Lohl's arena. Their executioner was to be the undefeated champion of seven years—Lunen.

However, upon seeing Liana's father stand defiant in his chains, determined to keep his daughter safe, much like his own father had done for him, Lunen made an appeal to Lohl, asking that he not be forced to make an orphan of the girl so close to his own age. Lohl responded by tossing the head of Lunen's mother into the arena.

The powers of the Gold moon were so potent that even in death, those who had claim to its light decayed slowly. Based on the decayed flesh and withered hair, Lunen believed Lohl when he said that he had executed her after Lunen's first match.

"He killed her?" Winnie's words were barely a whisper. "But I thought you had a deal…"

"As did I," Lunen replied, taking a deep breath. Wind-hunter slowly approached and gently nudged Lunen's head, his green eyes staring softly at the Triblood. "What Lohl expected was that, upon learning that I had fought for years for no purpose, I would break down and finally be just another slave."

"You don't strike me as the type who would just take something like that."

"Exactly."

He laughed. Tears of sadness streaked his face, but Lunen laughed as he cradled his mother's head. At first all those present, from Lohl and his guests to Liana and the rest of the crew of the *Freewind*, thought that he had gone mad.

Then his hands erupted in flames, incinerating his mother's head. The ashes scattered to the wind and danced in the sky. For a moment he looked at peace, despite the slowly-healing burnt flesh on his palms. Then he roared in grief and rage and charged the wall. In one great leap, Lunen was in the stands, rushing toward Lohl's private booth. Chaos ensued as the crew of the *Freewind* battled the guards. During the battle, Liana's father died protecting her from a hail of arrows.

And through it all, Lunen kept running. Lohl, in his arrogance, ordered his brigade of full Red-moon guards to attack Lunen instead of making an escape. It did no good. The Triblood would not be stopped. When they stabbed him, he tore out the blades and kept moving as the wound closed. He struck some guards with such force that the sound of their breaking bones formed a macabre orchestra. Others he did worse with that rare power of the North. Bodies burned in one moment and wind tore them apart the next. Water floated from discarded goblets, freezing men's heads with its touch before blows strong enough to break trees shattered them. Some men were thrown backward as bolts of lightning tore through them.

At last Lunen stood before Lohl. The greasy, overweight pig of a man trembled as Lunen stared at him with contained rage, his pasty skin flushed with terror as his beady grey eyes welled with tears. With a speed only capable of one with blood of the Red desert, the Triblood stabbed his fingers into Lohl's chest. As the flames began to do their damage within him, he realized the truth. Lunen was never his prisoner, never his slave. The Triblood had always been his death, held back only by a promise of safety and freedom for his mother. And as his body ignited from the inside out, Lohl cursed the day he thought he could control such a creature with a lie.

"After I killed Lohl, I took back the only things I had left of my parents," Lunen finished, reaching down his shirt. "This pendant was my mother's." He pulled out a solid metal pendant with two symbols for infinity interlinked, held around his neck by a metal chain. "And you've already seen my father's," he added, pointing to his dagger.

"Life is never perfect," Winnie responded, wiping tears from her eyes.

"Why would you say that?" Lunen asked, his eyes showing concern. "You're born and you die. Everything in between is always fifty/fifty." He shifted awkwardly, clearly not used to encouraging someone. "What more can you ask for than that?"

"What happened after all that?" Winnie asked, not sure if she should tell him anything about her own problems. She was sure it would seem like nothing compared to what he had been through.

"I felt obligated to join Liana's crew, since my riot killed her father. At first only Leito liked Wind-hunter and me. The others distrusted the crazy Triblood. Six years later, I'm still here, and I've more than proven my worth to those that count." He pulled a blanket up to his chest. "Now we should sleep. We got a big delivery to drop off tomorrow."

The longer I stayed around him, the more he made me feel so small. While I was trying to run away from my own problems, he faced his with a will of iron. Even in failure to protect his mother, he kept on persisting. To this day, I still don't know how he does it. The Triblood Lunen, I was starting to learn, was at his core someone who simply did not know how to give in, even in the face of overwhelming despair. No matter what, he seemed to try to just be the best, regardless of the things that gnawed at him from within.

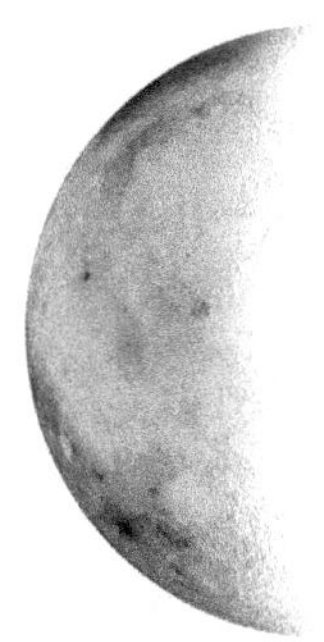

CHAPTER 3: The Pocket War

On that world with three moons, the people initially divided territory by which moon land was under. They then distributed it among those who tried to claim the land as though it were a prize and not simply what they walked upon. The Red and Gold moons orbited in perfect positions over the centers of the main continents while the Blue moon circled in a strange oval pattern around the Northern pole. The ancients thought this was because the Blue, unlike his siblings, became impatient waiting for the sun's return.

And it was believed among the rest of the world that those living on the Southern continent, known among them as the Frozen wastes, cursed the heavens. No moon orbited there, and with that came none of the powers that those in the North took for granted. In times long past, the tribes would send their children off to find someone to marry from the Gold or Red-moon lands in order to bring some of that power. But fate was cruel, for even if children were born with a foreign parent's powers, they could never have a moon of their own to pass to their own children, unless they were born under one of the moons themselves. So in time the Southern people cut almost all ties with those living under a moon's light, only making contact to trade.

Upon hearing of this history, Winnie had to ask, "So why are we going there again?"

The *Freewind* was past the point known as the Light-line, where any ship, whether on the ocean below or in the clouds as they were, could still see one of the moons. To the south stood a land of glowing white, where snow and ice came together to make a beautiful terrain, dangerous to the unprepared.

"Liana said she'd tell us when we were close enough, but I'm willing to bet it had to do with those Southerners she brought on board," Lunen replied.

As if on cue, Liana appeared from her cabin located near the rear of the ship. Leito followed her, as did the two Southern men, whom Winnie noted as being among the few people she'd met in this world who bore features similar to the Native Americans on her own world. They wore thick grey furs and their ebony hair braided.

The crew had been restless since hearing they were heading South. They had no fear of the terrain, for they had traveled most of the world. They avoided the South and North for only two reasons: the Blue-mooners of the North would probably kill them for entering their land without permission, and the Frozen wastes held very little profit.

Lunen sat on the starboard side's guardrail, his legs crossed. To his right, Winnie leaned against the rail holding a mop. She had tied her auburn hair into a ponytail. Lunen had discarded his mop to the ground as soon as the crew began to gather. Wind-hunter slept curled up next to the water buckets they were using. Migs and Zeg stood at the bottom of the stairs leading from the main deck to the upper section, where Liana's quarters were located. Just above that was the main steering apparatus for the ship: a large rudder that could have been made from tree trunks. By pulling and twisting it, one could change the direction the ship faced, to rise or drop. Sadly Winnie had yet to build the strength in her arms to a level where she could turn the ship by herself.

"*Why are we heading south?*" one crewman yelled from the throng. Winnie remembered his voice from the port where he had joined the crew simply because he did not wish to be caught by soldiers for petty theft. He was also among the minority of crew members who gave her and Lunen dirty looks, as if they were less than nothing.

"We have a job!" Liana cried out for them all to hear. "A job that promises to pay us in something worth its weight in gold!"

A murmur went up among the crew as they contemplated this.

"You mean we're going to get lots of thura meat?" Lunen asked with a smirk.

Liana gave him a glare as if he'd spoiled some big surprise. At this, the murmuring became excited whispers.

Winnie had had the privilege of eating thura meat with Lunen once. However, all she got was a small piece of meat only big enough to match the kind often skewered on a stick with some vegetables. After eating it, she learned two things: that it was possibly the most delicious meat in the world and that it was literally worth its weight in gold.

"That's right," Winnie said aloud. "You did say that thura meat came from an animal that only lived in the South."

"Yeah," Lunen said. "Now the question is, how much thura meat do they plan to pay us?"

"These people come from a village fortunate enough to be near one of the most densely populated areas where the thura beasts live," Liana said. "They make their living selling thura meat to the nobility in the Golden lands!" Liana let the crew put it all together in their minds. The nobility could afford to buy thura meat by the full size of a thura beast. A thura beast was twelve feet tall and weighed approximately five hundred pounds. And if this village sold thura meat to more than one noble house, that meant that the job could pay the *Freewind* well over a thousand pounds in gold if they sold the meat they receive instead of eating it.

"This explains why she took the job," Winnie commented, having learned that Liana was very much a savvy woman when it came to money, "but she still hasn't said what the job is."

"You're learning, Winnie," Lunen said, his smile vanishing as the crewman who'd started the shouting began again.

"*What kinda job is so horrible that they want to pay that much for it?*" he yelled.

"Please, let me speak," said the elder of the two Southern men. "My name is Far-blade, and this is my son, Snow-runner. We came because we needed help. The Empire sent an emissary to our village, demanding that we fly their banners and bow our heads to the Masked Emperor."

Winnie had heard the name of the enigmatic leader of the Empire often. She once asked Lunen why he was called simply "Masked Emperor." Lunen replied that no one had ever seen his true face behind a black clay mask, and even his birth name had never been spoken by anyone.

"Our village is small compared to the Empire, but our pride would not let us submit to them," Far-blade continued. "So the emissary left, promising that the might of the Imperial Army would rain down upon us in a month." Far-blade brought his hand up to his face to wipe a tear, trying to compose himself. "Our time is nearly up, and my son and I have traveled from port to port, hoping to hire someone to aid us in the defense of our village. Please, I beg of you, help us." He bowed his head to the crew, as did his son.

"To hell with that!" the same gruff voice from the crew yelled. "Why should we risk our lives to help some stupid no-moons?"

Suddenly the crew became a mass of shouting anger. The minority of the crew was angry at being drafted into what seemed to be a suicide mission for people they had no reason to care about, while the majority was enraged by the fact that these upstarts would dare challenge not just the authority of the captain but also the integrity of the *Freewind.*

"Will everyone stop acting like *children*?" Liana screamed. The arguing ended. "I have to agree, it does seem like a suicide mission. So I'm going to ask, if any of you think we can successfully pull this off, speak now."

Winnie groaned internally, because she knew one person who would be more than willing to say they could do it.

"I don't just think we can succeed," Lunen said. "I think we can make the Empire wish they never heard of this ship."

The screaming began again, but this time the minority directed their rage at Lunen.

"Why should we let a filthy damned Triblood have any say in what we do?" the same voice cried.

He stormed forward to confront Lunen, giving Winnie her first good look at him, and stopped short when Wind-hunter lifted his head to glare at him. The man's pink skin had flushed a bright red, making his bald head look to Winnie like a clown's nose. His pale handlebar mustache was not helping the comical effect of his appearance, and she giggled.

"Did I say something funny?" he barked at her.

"Yes, you asked why a man who has been on this crew years longer than you would have anything to say that matters more," Lunen replied with a smirk.

"Didn't know that men were born from cowards and whores," the bald man answered, turning away.

"You see this, Winnie?" Lunen said loud enough for all to hear. "He constantly attacks with words because, like any coward, he knows better than to fight someone who can easily kill him seven different ways."

The bald man stopped and turned to face Lunen.

"Fear benefits a man nothing," Lunen continued, this time glaring at the man, his voice becoming edged with a growl, "yet this fool would have you think that we should turn down a decent job because we have to fight the Empire's army."

"Is there a reason you want to die?" the bald man asked, reaching for his knife.

"Far-blade!" Lunen yelled to the old man, "How many in your village?"

"About five hundred able to use their spears," the old man replied.

"With us helping, that brings the number to over seven hundred, and that's not taking into account that we have Zeg's genius with explosives, or Liana and Leito's gift with strategy. And, of course, I *am* a Triblood, so I can do this." With that, Lunen flicked a pea-sized ball of fire at the troublemaker, forcing him to jump back. "So I think we should take the job, dive in headfirst, and see just how high we can raise the bounty on our heads, because honestly, I'm tired of being worth only two hundred gold pieces alive."

The crew started laughing, and the troublemaker stormed off. Liana smiled, knowing that she would now face no opposition to taking this job. Lunen was often the first to support her, and he never allowed insult to the captain to pass unpunished.

"You really think we can win against an army?" Winnie asked, dipping her mop into the bucket.

"I'll let you know when we get there," Lunen said with a sheepish grin.

Winnie sighed and thought, *I don't know how he can sound so impressive when he's just bullshitting his way through things.*

The *Freewind* was a special ship, built in that rare style that allowed it to land on both water and land. This was fortunate because it meant that Liana could keep the ship close to the village and avoid any complications that may arise from evacuation. When questioned about why she would plan to evacuate, she replied, "You really think I'm stupid enough to cut off my foot while drawing my sword?"

Winnie chose to accept this as a reasonable response and decided to preoccupy herself with checking out the village. It was set in a large, deep snow ditch. Huge stones had been placed around the perimeter to keep the snow from burying it whenever the wind blew. A towering pole in the middle of the village rose above them, and eight slightly smaller poles led from the top of the large one to the snow at the perimeter, ending at the four corners of the village's ditch and at the midpoints between those corners. Swathes of heavy canvas were bundled at the top of the main pole. The canvas would cover and protect the village during a snowstorm. Large tents lay scattered around the area, making it seem more like an Arabian caravan than what she'd imagined.

"What did you expect them to sleep in?" Lunen asked when she seemed shocked at the tents.

"Honestly, I was hoping to see igloos," she replied, tightening the fur coat around her.

"What the hell are igloos?" Lunen asked. He wore a black hooded cloak, which, he explained, was all he needed. He never really felt too warm or cold because of his Blue-moon.

"They're like little houses made out of ice by people on my world who live in areas like this," Winnie said. She never spoke about her being from another world to anyone except Lunen, simply because he seemed to figure that out when they met.

"Out of ice?" he asked. "Like this?" He extended his hands to the ground, the muscles on his arms tightening, and he bent his elbows in a quick snapping motion, bringing his hands up. As he did, the snow around him erupted, and a cylinder of ice surrounded him.

"That's amazing," Winnie said in awe.

"Yeah, except now I'm stuck."

"Why don't you just melt the ice then?"

"Think about it, Winnie," he answered in an annoyed voice. "Snow melts faster than ice. The heat I'd need to melt this ice would take the snow out from under me, and it's already unstable because I used the snow below to make this ice. Ice doesn't just come from nowhere, you know. Even a child Red-mooner knows that."

Winnie decided that borrowing one of the Southern people's pickaxes and tossing it into the cylinder was all the help he deserved after that tirade.

She gazed toward the Northern shore, taking note of the two hills flanking the village on that side. A small river flowed in the distance, and the bright sun hung in the sky.

She then turned as she heard the sound of ice shattering.

"So is this one of those areas that experiences daylight for a year?" she asked Lunen.

"Yes," he replied, turning the pickaxe over in his hands. "This little climbing tool has so many possibilities."

"Lunen! Winnie!" Leito's voice called. He also wore thick furs as he stood outside the council tent, the largest tent in the village, where Liana and the village leaders were speaking. "Go with some of the men and help bring in a thura beast for dinner! You could use the exercise!"

"Yes sir!" they both replied.

After two weeks, Winnie had gotten used to taking orders from Leito, something she would've expected to be more annoyed at. When she told Lunen this, he answered, "You aren't annoyed by it because Leito never asks you to do anything pointless."

About ten members of the crew accompanied twenty of the young men of the village, led by Snow-runner, as they slowly climbed down a large ice wall to the mouth of the river, where the thura beasts gathered. Lunen and Winnie watched from the top as the loud one who had insulted them earlier tried desperately not to fall.

"At least we have a faster way," Lunen commented before bringing his fingers to his lips, making a shrill whistle. Moments later, they heard the sound of leather wings as Wind-hunter swooped down to land next to Winnie.

"You're kidding," she said.

"Don't worry. He's more than capable of flying with someone on him."

Winnie placed one leg tentatively over the large cat's back, then pulled both her feet off the ground. "Wait. You said 'some-*one*.' How are we going to pull off two?" she asked.

"Who said anything about two?" Lunen replied with a grin, reaching down to grip the corners of his cloak. "After all, easiest element for a Blue-mooner to learn is the wind."

And with that, he dived off the cliff. Winnie felt Wind-hunter brace himself, and then they followed Lunen. She screamed until the sky-lynx's wings unfurled, and she felt the rhythmic dip-and-lift as he flapped them. She could never describe the feeling of joy she had as those wings made the air seem solid, like stepping from invisible stone to stone. Then she turned to watch Lunen. He simply glided along, his feet perfectly straight beneath him, his face a picture of peace. When he was about twenty feet off the ground, he let go of the cape and dropped into the snow. Wind-hunter dived and folded his wings, landing in a run.

"Now that's the only way to fly!" Lunen laughed. And, despite herself, Winnie laughed too.

They continued on foot to the river's mouth. The villagers were excited by the fact that one from the distant Blue-moon was among them, and that he had such a magnificent beast. The ten crewmen were used to Lunen's antics, and they disgusted at least one man.

"Sure, you can all gawk at the Triblood," the troublemaker sneered. "Just remember, he's the mark of shame for his family. Only traitors ever have Triblood children."

"Is it just me, or is his voice getting melodic, like a song your mother sings so often you don't even remember the words?" Lunen joked, giving Winnie a slight elbow.

"Laugh now, Triblood, but one day, I'm going to fix you the way you deser…"

Suddenly, a silver-skinned beast dropped from the sky, grabbing him with its arms. Its huge, transparent wings flapped quickly, creating a loud buzzing sound, as it ascended. The creature jabbed its narrow beak into the man's neck, and its throat gulped as it drained his blood. It then dropped the man to the ice-covered river, sending his body smashing clear through.

"What the hell is *that*?" Winnie cried out.

"A thura beast?" Lunen yelled to Snow-runner as more appeared. "I thought they only lived off water!"

"It must be their nesting season! They would only attack people to provide blood for the pregnant females. That's the only reason they'd be this hostile," the young hunter quickly replied as he and his fellows began notching arrows to their bows. The crewmen quickly pointed their spears to the sky.

"Well, don't we have all the luck?" Lunen said to no one in particular.

Thura beasts were large, silver, humanoid creatures with leather-like skin, egg-shaped heads, and gossamer wings. Their wide-set eyes were as sharp as they were black. Each had an unmoving hole for a mouth in the tip of its iron-hard beak. They lived off water in its various forms, which is why they thrived in the cold Southern continent.

Winnie had heard from Lunen how thura beasts were generally loners when they foraged, but incredibly strong. When hunting, the crux of any strategy was that you try to outnumber prey ten to one. She realized how much danger they were in when she saw eight more thura beasts swooping down to join the first. Arrows fired, spears stabbed, and Wind-hunter took to the skies to pounce on one. Red-mooners took to ripping chunks of ice from the ground to heave to the heavens, while Gold-mooners quickly shielded them.

A thura beast descended toward Winnie, the only one with no weapon, power, or experience of any kind, but Lunen shoved her to the ground, causing it to slam into him. Then it took off, the Triblood in its arms.

It had grabbed him around the waist, which he was thankful for. It left his arms free to draw his dagger. In a quick swing of his arm, he slashed its throat. Lunen fell as the thura beast released him to try to stop the blood flowing from its neck.

He quickly turned to face the ground and dived, aiming himself at the beast Wind-hunter was fighting. He brought his left hand to his lips and gave another shrill whistle. Wind-hunter removed his fangs from the thura beast's arm and flew away as Lunen slammed into it. Lunen had hoped that by hitting its back dagger-first, he would be able to damage the muscles that helped the wings move. Not for the last time was Lunen thankful for sheer dumb luck, because its wings twitched only once before they died. With that, they plummeted with increasing speed, smashing through the ice river and sending cracks to the distant shore.

Winnie picked up an injured man's spear and began swiping at the beasts as they came. One had nearly taken her from behind, but the thura beast with its throat slashed crashed on top of it.

I might actually survive this, she thought. But then she saw the distant sun. More large silver shapes blotted it out.

The ice in the river exploded, forcing both humans and thura beasts to stop their battle. Lunen pulled himself from the waters gasping, his teeth chattering. He ripped the wet cloak from his body and glared at all the sky-borne creatures. "Hey, Winnie!" he called out through clenched teeth, his fingers twitching with barely-contained rage. "You ever see a wind-cut before?"

He brought his right hand across his chest, his index and middle fingers extended. Winnie stared, unsure what he was planning. Then he whipped his arm out, and the air in front of him became distorted in the shape of an arc. Winnie watched the arc move through the sky at an incredible speed until it struck one of the thura beasts, decapitating it.

Lunen quickly repeated the motion with his open left hand and followed that with a diagonal swipe of his open right, then a horizontal swipe of his left. In the sky, invisible blades severed thura beasts as many more turned to escape that which they did not understand.

But Winnie understood. For reasons beyond her, she excelled in her science lessons. *He's using his Blue-mooning to make a mobile vacuum in an arc with his hands, using the fingers to change the width. When the vacuum reaches something solid, it draws it in quickly to fill the void, ripping whatever it touches apart in a clean slice.*

She turned to look at him, unsure how to react to surviving what she'd been certain would be her last moments. Then she saw the thura beast he had crashed with rise from the water behind him. She quickly gave a shrill whistle. As Wind-hunter swooped near her, she leapt onto him.

Lunen turned as he heard the water shift behind him. His hand quickly went for his dagger, but it was not at his hip. The beast lurched forward, forcing him to dive backward. This was a good decision on his part as Winnie, her spear pointed forward like an ancient jouster, rode Wind-hunter into the thura beast. Her spear snapped as she pushed into it, and she fell face first onto the cracked ice. Her arms stung with the recoil of the crash. She could taste the copper flavor of blood from her cut lip, and her head throbbed.

She heard the ice slowly break beneath her and turned, facing the creature. Before it could attack, arcs of lightning shot through its body and it fell to the ground. Lunen had leapt onto its back, his fingers wrapped around his dagger, still lodged in the beast, making it easier to electrocute it. He gave Winnie a smile as he stumbled to his feet.

"You just had your first victory, Winnie," he said in a congratulatory voice.

"This is what I've been *eating*?" she screamed, pointing hysterically to the creature he stood on.

"The sad thing is, you'll still want to eat more," he replied.

Winnie opened her mouth to shout back at Lunen. She stopped and pouted. He was right.

Liana smiled as they returned, carrying the severed bodies of the thura beasts. The villagers rushed from their tents to watch. They were fortunate enough if they caught three beasts, and the hunting party had returned with twelve. Lunen strode forward, his body wrapped in the cloak he had dried with his Blue-mooning, Winnie and Wind-hunter flanking him.

"Such a thing has never been seen in these parts," Far-blade said to Leito as they stood outside the council tent with Liana.

"Neither have sky-lynxes or Tribloods," Leito replied with a chuckle, unsurprised at how things had played out.

"All right, I need everyone to strip the bones so we can shape them into weapons," Liana called out. She then spied Winnie's bruised forehead and split lip. "What happened?"

"Well, I did something really stupid…" Winnie began.

"She charged a thura beast while riding Wind-hunter to save me," Lunen replied with a smirk, his impressed tone not really hiding the concern his eyes showed due to her injuries. "It was perfect, until she was knocked down."

"Shut up!" she yelled, her face flushing with embarrassment.

"A spear, eh?" Leito asked. "You strike me more as a staff kind of woman."

"Why would you think that?" Winnie asked, nervous about where this was going.

"You have no killing edge," Lunen answered with a strange tone in his voice. "Leito, you think you could teach her some of your little stick arts?"

"Stick arts?" Leito roared, his hand vanishing beneath his furs. Strapped to his back always was his weapon: a folding pole-arm, which folded at three points. The metal staff portion of the weapon was seven feet in length, and the one-foot-long blade at one end brought the entire weapon to a length of eight feet. And now all eight feet of it were pointed at Lunen.

"Wait! Wait, I'm sure he didn't mean…" Winnie attempted to interject, but she knew it probably would not help. Leito was like Liana's father; with two-and-a-half Red-moons in his blood, his physical strength enormous, and he was incredibly skilled. Even Lunen could not strike fast enough to stop him from at least taking a limb from his position.

"So, you going to teach her or not?" Lunen asked.

"Sure. I have time," Leito smirked, turning to face Winnie. "When I'm through with you, you're going think of your weapon as an extension of your body."

Damn you, Lunen! Winnie thought as she saw him chuckling to himself.

*****

"I just can't believe Lunen did that to me, Migs!" Winnie yelled as the doctor applied a salve to her lip.

"You do realize if you keep talking, your saliva will not allow the salve to heal you," he replied plainly.

They sat on the snow near the large council tent. A meeting was about to take place between the village and the crew. That was the only reason that two hours of training at Leito's hands had ended. Her new staff, just fashioned from thura bone, already showed the scratches and marks of repeated use. Her arms screamed within her skin each time she moved them as traitorous muscles stopped short of anything she wanted.

"I swear, I'm going to kill him if he makes one joke about this," she growled, allowing Migs to help her up.

"Considering how minor your injuries, he should not overreact as he has," he commented.

"What are you talking about?" she asked as they passed through the huge tent flaps.

"If your injuries were more severe, it would make more sense for him to ask Leito to teach you to protect yourself. Then again, his logic never did make much sense to me."

As she sat down between the twins inside the large tent, Winnie decided she would look at the pain in her limbs as something to be appreciative about.

"Far-blade," the eldest man in the village said loud enough for all present to hear, "we sent you and your son to bring us help. While we are grateful for *this* crew you have brought us, could you have not brought three more?"

Laughter filled the tent. He meant no insult; he only phrased his words as such because of the fear gripping them.

"But what a crew we found!" Snow-runner exclaimed. "Brave and resourceful. And one of them was able to kill several thura beasts with no weapons!"

Winnie scanned the crowd, looking for Lunen's smug grin, but found that he was absent.

"Still, even with their aid, we do not number in the thousands, as our enemies may," the elder said, running his hand through his beard.

"That may be the case," Liana said from her place before the elder, "but the only people from our lands who come here are traders. They may be trained for war, but I doubt they're ready to battle you in a land they've never set foot upon, especially one where you all have grown."

"And the terrain isn't our only advantage," Leito added from his seat to Winnie's right. "Every man here is a hunter. They already know how to work together and how to kill from their experiences against the thura beasts. We need only teach them how to adapt their tactics to fight Red-mooners and Gold-mooners."

"Don't forget the one who brought down so many thura!" a voice called from the villagers.

"Yes, with him, surely no foe could beat us!" another added.

"Where is that fight-happy little moron anyway?" Liana asked.

"*Migs!*" Lunen called from outside.

Everyone rushed out of the tent. Winnie was nearly thrown to the ground in the stampede.

"Hang on, missy!" Zeg said as he caught her by the arms. "Wouldn' want ya trampled, now would we?"

Winnie smiled at the short engineer, and then they hurried outside and pushed their way through the crowd. Her breath caught in her throat when she saw Lunen on his knees, Wind-hunter lowering his head as the Triblood cradled one of the Southern men, a boy who looked no older than fifteen. His blood stained the snow red.

"That's Ice-skipper!" someone cried.

"No!" Snow-runner screamed, rushing toward the youth.

"What's going on?" Liana asked.

"We sent a scouting group to one of the far cliffs to watch for the coming Imperials," the elder said.

"Wind-hunter took off after a scent he picked up earlier," Lunen said. "I followed, and we found this boy stumbling back to the village."

"Brother?" the boy said as Snow-runner cupped his hand.

"It's me, you little fool," Snow-runner said, tears running from his eyes. His father stood behind him. "Save your breath."

"I have so little left, I should probably make it useful," Ice-skipper said with a weak smile. "A large black ship that could not fly... So many men stood on its deck, and that was only the deck...and the man with mad eyes...He looked at us, and the snow beneath us became pikes of ice...Everyone died, while I felt my life leave me through my belly...It would take them a week to move their boat to the coast closest to us...I'm so sorry, Father..."

"You have nothing to feel sorry for, my son," Far-blade said, refusing to let his grief choke his words.

Snow-runner's body heaved as he sobbed, feeling his younger brother's grip loosen until at last he was gone.

"Damn them," Liana cursed under her breath. "They sent a small army. Only reason to send a ship too big to fly."

"The Imperial army is made of the most dangerously trained men in this world," Leito said slowly. "Every last one of them has been trained for years to decimate whatever they're pointed at, and since their members are from both the Gold and Red continents, it'll be a hard battle, to face them all and survive."

"It is said," Migs said, choosing his word carefully, "that one ship of that type can carry close to fifty thousand, all trained and eager to fight."

"And their leader has to be Imakur," Lunen said, rising to his feet after giving the dead boy to his brother, "an exile from the Blue lands with three full Blue moons in his blood. He is the right hand of the Masked Emperor, the general of his best forces, and he is fond of killing with his powers. He's the only one who could have killed the scouting party in such a way."

Both crew and villagers stood in silence. Fear had gripped them by their hearts, and they were no longer certain there was any hope.

"I say we no longer simply fight," Liana said through clenched teeth. "I say we make them suffer."

"We still have the terrain," Leito cried, "and we still have the time to prepare for them!"

"I will not run and leave my brother's soul in unrest," Snow-runner said.

"And I just happen to have something special planned for them fools!" Zeg added.

"The Empire has made a huge mistake!" Liana yelled, letting the crowd's growing hope and anger fuel her words. "Before, you only wanted to defend your home, and we only came to help you in that. Now they've given us a reason to be angry, and the only thing more dangerous than a free human being defending their home is an angry one!"

The crowd screamed declarations of war to the sky, their fear gone like a sheet of ice down a river. Winnie felt in her blood that she would not be turned back. She felt a hand on her shoulder.

"We're going to have to step up your training," Leito said to her.

Lunen drew his dagger and thrust it toward the sky, and they all sounded their wordless battle cry for the approaching forces to hear from that day into eternity, his words summing up their joined feelings: "*We're going to make them remember the day they came south!*"

During that week in the land where the sun would not set for another few months, the preparations for the coming battle were quick and intense. The first day at "morning," those who would fight awoke. Lunen, already up, had used his command over the snow and ice to make a veritable army of practice dummies for them to hone their skills on. After the morning meal, all assembled in the council tent for Liana to explain various strategies. Yet afterward, all assembled felt that nothing would help against the sheer numbers they faced.

Leito, overseen by Liana, continued to train Winnie and gave the small army of defenders their exercises in spears. For hours until their lunchtime, Winnie practiced striking with both ends of a staff, spinning and swinging it to put her enemies at a distance, and ducking and falling with the weapon so that even on her back she could fend off attackers.

Why am I still doing this? I'm not a fighter. The thought entered her mind often. Yet when it did, she would look to where Lunen was training. Ever since he first held the pickaxe in his hand, he'd been trying to understand how he could take a climbing tool and use it as a weapon. During those hours before their "afternoon" meal, he practiced striking at an opponent's vitals or hooking one of their limbs with one pickaxe in each hand. Since saving him on the ice, a part of Winnie had wanted to catch up with him in terms of skill.

"Why would you ever think of using a pickaxe like that?" she asked him during lunch.

"It's sorta like a habit I've had since the arena," he answered, taking a large bite of thura meat. "I guess when you grow up having to know what can be used as a weapon in a tight spot, you get used to it." He drank from a warm bowl of broth. "How goes your training?"

"Pretty good," she replied, smiling with honest pride. "I'm actually falling without hurting myself too much. How about you?"

"The pickaxes are good for very close quarters, but they'd need something to help them work at medium range."

"Too bad you can't just tie a rope to it and swing it around," she joked. She stopped smiling when she saw what could only be called inspiration flash in his eyes. She knew to be afraid when Lunen was inspired.

When they resumed training after lunch, many watched in awe as Lunen practiced with his new adaptations. He took a long length of rope and tied one end of it to a pickaxe. Then he tied the other end of the rope to his belt and began using it as he had in close range with his right hand, but he would then throw the tool and swing it by the rope, achieving the distance he sought. He demonstrated his proficiency with his new toy by decapitating one of the practice dummies from fifteen feet, swinging the pickaxe into its neck. And he still had the second pickaxe in his left hand for close quarters.

"Wouldn't it be easier to just throw fireballs at them?" Winnie called from where she was training.

"And risk hitting one of ours?" he answered with a satisfied look as he continued to swing his pickaxe around. "Besides, it's been a long time since I used whip-like weapons. I need the practice."

He doesn't think he might hit somebody with that too? Winnie wondered.

The "evening" concluded with the small army practicing their archery on the dummies that still stood. Leito drilled it into their minds to aim for the head. If their targets turned out to be Goldmooners, nothing short of a fatal attack to the head would stop them.

"How goes the preparation?" Migs asked Winnie as he approached the training grounds.

"Seems all right, all things considered," she answered, thankful for the break. "Are you planning to fight?"

"I am a field medic by training," Migs answered, bringing up his right hand, covered in a white glove. Winnie noticed for the first time that he wore a ring on each finger of that glove.

"What does that have to do with it?" she asked, feeling a sense of foreboding from those rings.

Migs smiled, something she rarely saw him do outside the presence of his twin during one of their better sessions together. His half-moon spectacles flashed as his hand whipped out toward one of the practice dummies. What appeared to be five piano wires extended from his hand at incredible speed and wrapped around the ice figure. Migs then tightened his hand into a fist and quickly pulled it back, slicing the ice dummy perfectly into six pieces.

"It means I know how to defend myself during combat situations," he said as he pushed his glasses up with the index finger of his right hand.

Under other circumstances, Winnie would have been terrified by that display of skill. Yet, in preparation for the coming fight, she could only hope that having someone like Migs on their side could help against the sheer numbers.

Zeg, while absent from the training grounds, was not loafing on the job. After they had moved the *Freewind* to a position next to the village, its portside cannons aimed right where the enemy would approach from, he'd locked himself up in his lab near the gaianite engine. When Winnie earlier expressed concern at a lab being that close to the engine, Liana reassured her that her father did not let Zeg have a lab until he made sure it was reinforced enough that no accidents would affect the ship. That did not make it easier to ignore the occasional muffled *boom* during the preparations.

When Winnie brought Zeg his food, soot covered his red hair and his goggles were grimy. An ice block lay on his work table in the middle of the lab, and various glass tubes of chemicals sat scattered about, all tightly corked.

"Do I want to know what you've been up to?" she asked as she placed the thura meat and broth on one of the worktables.

"Ain't nuthin' wrong with curiosity, ya know!" he said with a laugh. He pointed to the ice block as he began to eat his food. "Ya see, the shore where the enemy is coming from starts with a large, thick sheet of ice, then it gets to the thicker, more stable ice that makes the ground under this place. And no matter how hot a fire is, it won't ever burn straight through one spot in ice without melting everything around it."

"Why would you want to burn straight through one spot?" she asked, taking a drink of what she'd decided was her favorite drink on this strange world, a juice that tasted like grape but came from a fruit that looked more like a coconut.

"If I could burn through a controlled spot in ice, maybe we could set a trap for them when they land. I just need to find the right combo of chemicals."

Winnie was never sure if prayer worked, but when she left Zeg, she silently hoped to heaven that he'd find the chemicals he needed.

Three days into the preparations, Winnie decided to ask Lunen something during lunch that she'd been afraid to ask. "Why haven't you asked me to not be here when the fighting starts?"

He gave her his worst look, the one where she could not read what he was thinking. "Do you not want to fight?" he asked.

"It's bad manners to answer a question with a question," she said with a nervous smile. "I'm terrified of this battle that's coming. I really don't want to die."

"But?" he said, sipping at his broth.

"But I saw that boy, and I see you and everyone preparing, and I don't want to be useless to the crew during this."

"I would prefer it if no one other than me had to fight," he said, looking into her blue eyes with his intense brown ones. "But everyone has to fight when they feel they must. I can't tell you what to do, Winnie. What I can tell you is that I'm going to watch out for you on that icy field like I've done since we first met."

She smiled. *He can't afford to be preoccupied with my safety. I need to get stronger,* she thought.

Word began to travel that there would be a snowstorm that evening.

"Maybe if we're lucky, it'll cut their numbers in half," Lunen said as he bit into a piece of boiled thura meat.

"Too bad those two hills aren't like Thermopylae. That'd make their numbers useless," Winnie said, staring into her broth.

"What are you talking about?" Lunen asked.

"That's right. You never heard of that battle on this world," she said. "Let's just say, according to the story, that there was once an army consisting of a million, marching on a country. One of the kings from that country under siege took only three hundred of his men, along with some volunteers, to face the invading army. They met at a place called Thermopylae, which meant 'Hot Gates' in their language. A huge mountain range with only one path through, it was narrow enough that for three days, the invading army's numbers meant nothing. They lost soldiers by the thousands. I just thought that if those hills were like Thermopylae, we could make fifty thousand useless against our seven hundred."

As she spoke, Lunen listened. As she told him more, his eyes widened and his mouth opened. When she stopped, he had a look of insanity, as if he couldn't believe his luck.

"Why are you looking at me like that?"

"Who won?" he asked.

"Don't answer a question with a question, remember? Anyway the invaders killed the defenders, but that was just because one of the locals betrayed them and led the enemy around so that they could attack from both sides of the mountain. Why?"

Lunen stood and quickly ran to where the elder sat. She couldn't hear what was said, but she saw the elder's surprised face as Lunen leapt into the air and screamed in sheer joy. He then ran back to her. "Winnie, you may have just saved us all," he said with a big smile.

Word spread through the village that Lunen and Winnie had found a way to make the enemy's size worthless. After lunch, the two were brought into the council tent, where Liana, Leito, and the elder waited to hear it.

"How did you get me involved in this?" Winnie asked through clenched teeth.

"Just tell them what you told me," Lunen replied in the same manner.

And so Winnie told the story of Thermopylae again, and this time it was Leito and Liana who reacted as if she had somehow given them a chicken that laid golden eggs.

"The reports of the snowstorm," Liana asked, "are they true?"

"Yes," said the elder, "but I don't see why you all seem so happy."

"Lunen may only have one full Blue in him, sir," Leito replied, "but a snowstorm would send enough snow into the air for him to use the winds to gather it."

"He could then shape them in the sky into anything he wanted before they land," Liana added.

"And if I could use those two hills as starting points to make a large mountain of ice, with a narrow tunnel the only way to the village…" Lunen said, leaving the idea hanging in the air.

"Then you could make their numbers mean nothing!" Winnie gasped as she realized just what she'd set in motion.

"How would you survive out in the storm, away from our protective canvas?" the elder asked.

"Do you have clothing that is warm, but doesn't take one's speed from him?" Lunen asked.

"Yes, made from thura skin, with fur lining the inside," the elder replied.

"That's all I'll need!"

Lunen stood outside the canvas dressed in thura leather. Silver and tough, it covered his entire body. The coat even had a hood, which he pulled up over his head and tightened. He tied a piece of cloth around his nose and mouth so he could breathe easier. His hands were gloved, but he could still feel the outside world enough to affect it. The winds had pushed snow high enough that his feet crunched though the white surface up to his knees. Clouds and swirling white mist blotted out the sun.

He was thankful as he pulled his mother's pendant out from beneath his clothing to kiss, thankful for the skills he had and thankful for being in a position to help these people. And he was thankful for Winnie being there. If she had not told him that story, he was certain he would never have thought of this plan.

Lunen raised his open hands to the sky. He focused on the muscles in his arms and his legs, on the snow and the wind, and on his beating heart, which he willed not to falter during this task. Then he was off.

His feet kicked up fresh fallen snow as they barely touched it before moving to the next step. His speed increased as his arms fell behind him, calling the wind to follow with its airborne cargo of snow. He approached the hill to the right and leapt, calling to the snow to obey him. He willed the snow to become colder and more tightly packed, begging it to become what he saw in his mind. As he landed, he brought both fists into the top of the hill and heard the sounds of solid mass taking shape. He looked at what he had created.

The top the hill had become solid ice. It also slowly crept along the sides toward the bottom. The ice grew off the hill's original summit and angled to create what he hoped would be an arc toward the other hill. Then he saw the height it had gained: a mere three meters.

"It's a start," Lunen said to himself, the smile beneath his makeshift scarf obvious to any who could have heard his voice.

As the storm raged on for three hours, Winnie and Windhunter stayed near the only entrance into the village through the canvas. They fought fatigue, both silently promising the other that they would not sleep until they saw Lunen again.

They leapt to attention when they finally heard that shrill whistle, and both led the villagers and crew outside. The first thing they saw was a huge mountain of solid ice rising so steeply toward the sky that no army could scale it without the proper equipment and preparations. The two hills of snow now served as the two lowest points of the mountain that had sprung up in a matter of hours. And at the bottom of the mountain, a circular tunnel roughly eight feet in diameter went through its center. Their enemies would not be able to pass moving more than two at a time through it.

"Where's Lunen?" Winnie asked aloud.

"Where's the snow that usually builds up around our perimeter?" Snow-runner added.

Then they all heard a barbaric scream from the top of the canvas. Their eyes quickly rose to see Lunen in his thura coat, standing atop the great pole towering above the center of the village, his hands stretched up toward the heavens. Above him, all the snow that had built up at the foot of their canvas hung in the air, suspended by his will. With another loud scream, he threw his arms forward, sending the snow shooting through the air to hit the ice mountain. Within moments, only the tunnel remained visible. Lunen had used the built-up snow to make the mountain look as natural as possible. His job complete, he fell forward, skidding down the canvas before crashing onto the ground.

"Migs!" Winnie screamed as she ran to Lunen. The doctor quickly joined her as he assessed the damage.

"His hands are frozen," he said under his breath. "What happened to your gloves?"

"C-couldn't work the w-w-winds or s-snow as well w-with g-gloves," Lunen said through chattering teeth. "N-n-n-needed to f-finish the job."

"Can you make a ball of fire between your hands?" Migs asked. Lunen did as he asked, resting his head against Winnie's lap. His fingers involuntarily twitched as blood and warmth returned to them.

"Lunen has improved our chances!" Snow-runner yelled. "Let's make sure not to waste it!" The villagers cheered, and, as they went inside the canvas to get their weapons for the day's training, they thanked the Triblood.

"Was that mountain always there?" Zeg chimed in as he approached the *Freewind* crewmembers surrounding Lunen.

"We'll explain later," Liana responded. "Anything to report?"

"I found the right combo!" Zeg said with a big smile.

"It seems that this small war of ours may go in our favor," Leito commented, a plan already forming in his mind.

"You actually did it," Winnie whispered. "You made Thermopylae."

"Wouldn't be one to make if you didn't tell me about it," Lunen said with a smile, ignoring the prickling pain of his frozen hands being warmed by the burning sphere he balanced between them.

The day had arrived, and the large black ship of the Imperial forces docked. The gangplanks lowered, and a mass of black forms descended. They were all human. That was all one could see, for their black armors and helmets revealed no skin or facial features. They held steel shields, swords, and spears with practiced ease, every one of them ready to take this insignificant village that bore no moon. So the surprise they felt at not only an unreported mountain blocking their path but a small group of people standing on the ice where they had docked was quite high.

Liana stood in the center of the group with Leito to her right and Lunen to her left. To Leito's right stood Snow-runner, and to Lunen's left, Winnie. Leito carried a large boulder on his shoulder, while Lunen twirled his pickaxes in anticipation. All wore thura leather boots, the claws of the beasts used as spikes so they could move freely on the ice, unlike the soldiers, who skidded and stumbled with each step.

"Where is your leader?" Liana said. "Where is Imakur?"

"I am here," a deep voice called with an air of arrogance. Their eyes rose to the ship, and they watched a man clad in regal black armor step over the side. Yet instead of falling, he continued to walk along the air as if on an invisible road. He stared at them with eyes that were pinholes within white orbs in the middle of his angular, bronzed face, his jet-black hair standing straight up like a bed of nails.

So that's the power of a Blue-mooner with three full moons, Winnie thought.

"I take it you are here to negotiate surrender?" he said, staring down at them.

"Yes, we accept your surrender," Lunen said with a chuckle. He fell silent when he saw Liana glare at him.

"Your dog needs more discipline," Imakur commented in a casual tone that made it difficult to tell whether Lunen's words angered him. "I do hope he does not speak for all of you?"

"No, he does not," Liana replied. "We're not interested in letting you surrender."

"You should mind your tongue, girl!" he yelled at her. "I am General Imakur of the Imperial Elite, leader of the greatest army in the world! Who are *you* to dare speak to me like this?"

"I am Liana, captain of the *Freewind*!" she replied with equal ferocity.

"Ah, the *Freewind*," Imakur said, a smile forming. "That would explain the new mountain. Which one of you is Lunen?"

"That'd be me," Lunen answered.

"Of course," Imakur said, his eyes focused on Lunen. "You look so much like your father, Kabern, on the day he caused my exile."

They all stared at Lunen, surprised that at the furthest point of the world, they could still find someone who wanted to kill the Triblood for an arbitrary reason.

"My father only stopped your attempt to take the Five Sages' lives. You were responsible for your own exile," Lunen replied, ignoring the stares.

"I was so disappointed when I heard he died," Imakur continued, "And when I found out his son escaped the arena, I was so sad that I'd never have a chance to kill you."

"Kill me?" Lunen said, stepping toward the army. "Thanks to your idiotic attempt to take power, I got to be taught by the Sages themselves as thanks to my father. You may have three full Bluemoons, but I can make flames more intense than you've ever been capable of."

Imakur roared, and thrust his hand at Lunen. A massive fist made of flame launched, twisting as it flew at the Triblood. Lunen grinned and leapt backward. The fist struck the ice, producing a spark. Suddenly, in a long arch, fire spread and burned in a concentrated line, along which they had poured Zeg's concoction earlier. The ice cracked loudly as the chemical fire cut the section that the first two hundred troops stood on, away from the mainland. Leito threw the boulder he carried into the air.

Using Snow-runner's spear for leverage, Liana leapt after the boulder. Her father's birth moon had been a full Red, and even if her mother, who died bringing her into this world, was born during a new moon like Liana herself, her strength still equaled what Lunen was capable of. She kicked the boulder with both legs, using it as a platform to leap back to the others.

The boulder smashed into the now-separated patch of floating ice, causing it to shatter beneath the black-clad soldiers' feet. As they floundered in the freezing water, Lunen stood at the edge where the fire had cut through. He thrust his hands out, still gripping their pickaxes, and the water froze again, now with the soldiers trapped in clusters of ice.

"Told you I could make better flames!" Lunen called to Imakur before he and the others took off running to the tunnel. The general's roar to his troops to kill them all echoed through the tunnel as they ran.

"Was it a good idea to piss him off?" Winnie asked as she took her position once they cleared the tunnel.

"If he can focus his anger, then no," Lunen said as he took his position. "But, given his arrogance, I doubt he'll be able to focus after that insult."

The sounds of marching echoed through the tunnels, as did the crunching sounds of boots stepping on snow. The march slowed within the newly formed mountain, for the soldiers had no experience fighting on ice. As they cleared the tunnel two at a time and set foot on the less slippery snow, they brought their spears up to charge—and that was the last thing those first soldiers did.

Perched on the inclines that had once been the hills, groups of archers guarded by warriors with spears and shields made from stretched thura skin waited. As soon as the soldiers began filing out, the arrows fell upon them. The arrowheads had spiraling tips so that the arrows spun like drills as they flew, giving them extra force to pierce the armor and shields of the enemy. But eventually the archers stopped to reload, and the soldiers pushed past the building mound of bodies.

Then phase three of Liana's plan began. Once the archers could no longer fire, the soldiers began to spill out, hoping to take advantage of their superior numbers, and that's when the bulk of the defending forces attacked. Lines of warriors charged into the soldiers who were no longer at the exit of the tunnel, spears and shields clashing.

In the midst of the battle, Winnie swung her staff and felt a satisfying *crack* as one soldier fell to the snow. She quickly turned and brought her weapon down across another soldier's knees, feeling them shatter.

"Doesn't look like they brought many Gold-mooners!" Liana called as she weaved through the soldiers. Her twin cutlasses kept her enemies at bay, and her claim proved true when soldiers she had merely slashed at their arteries fell, their wounds never closing.

"I guess the great Empire didn't have sense enough to bring people who could survive for long!" Leito called as he skewered one soldier with his pole-arm. He then grabbed another by the helmet and threw him into the oncoming crowd, knocking three more down.

"Looks like the archers are ready!" Snow-runner yelled as the archers fired a second volley at the tunnel's mouth, preventing reinforcements from aiding in the battle. The bodies continued to pile, making it a struggle for the soldiers to leave the tunnel.

Winnie continued weaving through the attacking soldiers, their numbers apparently stretched so thin they could not be bothered to outnumber her, something she was thankful for. *I'm also thankful to have...*

"Duck!" Lunen screamed. Winnie dropped to her knees while thrusting her staff forward, striking her opponent in the chin and sending him flying. Lunen's pickaxe sailed through the air. When the rope became taut, he swung into a soldier's shoulder, pulling him off his feet and dragging him in an arc before the blade pulled free from his body. If he had not warned her, that same soldier would have struck Winnie from behind.

Lunen quickly yanked his weapon back and waded into the soldiers. He became fond of a maneuver where he would hook a soldier by the leg with one pickaxe and then bring the other into his chest, pushing him down while puncturing his heart. After a minute of this, he came back to back with Winnie.

"Still think I should have kept you out of this?" he asked over his shoulder.

"If we live, I'll let you know!" she replied, smashing her staff against another soldier's helmet.

They kept fighting with their backs to each other, as if that was the natural order of the world. Neither born with any desire to be in such a huge battle, yet there they were, drawn by their principles and their belief in each other. And somehow, despite her inexperience and his usual preference to be on his own when he fought, Lunen and Winnie made a great team.

"Oh my God!" Winnie screamed when she saw a huge soldier, close to eight feet tall and possibly half as wide, charging them with a large axe.

They both dived to either side as the soldier brought his weapon down where they had stood. Lunen quickly leapt over him, making sure his pickaxe lodged in the giant's collarbone.

"How do you think he got through the tunnel?" Lunen asked in midair.

Winnie had rolled along the ground while Lunen took the higher path, her waist bending around her staff like Leito had taught her. As she uncurled from her roll, she prepared to swing her weapon at the back of the giant's feet.

"Definitely by himself!" she answered while swinging.

The soldier fell, his feet knocked out from beneath him as Lunen pulled him backward. As Lunen twisted in the air, his hands began to crackle with electricity. He brought his fists down on the black armor, and the soldier's body convulsed with the lightning coursing through him. Lunen looked disappointed, for his finishing blow had burned his pickaxes to the point of uselessness.

"I'm going to have nightmares about this battle, aren't I?" Winnie asked, catching her breath.

"If you didn't have nightmares after your first major battle, I'd be worried," Lunen replied, panting.

They both looked up to see a group of soldiers rushing toward them. And at the same time, they both sighed and brought their fingers to their lips. After twin shrill whistles, Wind-hunter appeared and scared the soldiers off. He turned to Lunen and Winnie, giving them a sad look.

"Come on; he's been cooped up since training began," Winnie pleaded.

"Oh, all right, but don't do anything stupid," Lunen told the sky-lynx before it bounded away after what foes remained. After a few more moments of catching their breath, they separated and rejoined the battle, Winnie pressing toward the tunnel while Lunen moved to the flanks to help Liana and Leito.

Villagers and crewmen suffered injuries during the course of the battle. And each time Migs would race to them, a satchel with his tools in hand. At first the soldiers attempted to attack him, but the wire glove he wore soon made it clear that the white-clad doctor was to be left alone. As such, he was the only one not preoccupied by combat, and it was he who shouted the warning.

"*Imakur!*" he cried, drawing several of the defenders' eyes to the sky, where the Blue-mooner raced upon his road of air, his cape swirling behind him. He landed with force near the mound of growing bodies just as the archers were beginning to reload and brought his hands up to face the tunnel.

"He's going to widen the tunnel! Stop him!" Liana ordered as she continued to fend off soldiers two at a time.

Snow-runner charged, his spear held high, the sight of his brother's blood still fresh in his mind. He thrust his arm out, and the spear sailed toward his target. Imakur quickly turned, and the wind concentrated with such force near him that it splintered the spear. The Blue-mooner smiled and pointed his crackling fingers at Snow-runner. As he prepared to fire, Imakur felt pain in his wrist, and his hand was suddenly pointed toward the sky as the lightning bolt launched. He turned his head to Winnie and saw her staff pressed against his throbbing hand. He thrust his open palm at her, and she found out what it was like to be caught in a hurricane wind. Yet she landed in a crouched position, her staff at the ready.

"You're truly a brave one," Imakur commented, cracking his knuckles.

"I'm not too sure about that," Winnie said, blood running down her cheeks from where the wind had cut her.

Lunen stood too far away to help when he saw Winnie facing Imakur—at least, too far to help without aid of his own. "Leito!" he called to the large first mate fighting at his side. "How's your aim?"

"Better than yours!" Leito said as he grabbed Lunen and threw him at Imakur. As the Triblood sailed through the air, he unsheathed his dagger and began to spin. The snow beneath him rose and began swirling around before compressing and freezing, taking shape. When it was done, Lunen had encased himself inside a giant flying ice spear.

Winnie saw the attack coming from over Imakur's shoulder and smiled. When Imakur turned to see what she was looking at, all he could see was a large, sharp ice projectile.

"The Triblood is creative; I'll give him that," he commented as he thrust his right palm at the glacial missile. It was his aim to shatter the ice and send the sharp shards back at Lunen, who he thought had launched it.

Imakur's smile turned to a stunned look as the ice shattered, revealing Lunen inside. Despite the shards cutting at his body, Lunen extended his left arm and gripped the Blue-mooner by his extended right wrist as he landed. He pulled and ducked, maneuvering Imakur and slashing the general's side with his dagger. His grip still firm on Imakur's wrist, Lunen brought his dagger into the Blue-mooner's shoulder blade. He then drew his dagger out and let go of Imakur's wrist, pivoting and punching the general with enough Red-moon strength to send him flying into the ice mountain's wall.

The soldiers did not know what to make of it. When things were dire, Imakur's presence usually changed the tide of battle. Yet they could all see him, blood staining the ice. His arm desperately needed medical attention.

"Retreat for now!" he roared before taking to the sky, his blood still flowing as he took off over the mountain. The troops were quick to follow his commands in fear—of both Imakur and the warriors who were defeating them.

Lunen smiled as they began to retreat, the cuts on his face and arms already closed with nothing but bloodstains proving they were ever there.

"*Don't you remember what the plan was if they retreated?*" Winnie yelled.

"Oh, damn," Lunen cursed under his breath before sheathing his dagger and scooping Winnie up in his arms. He then took off in a burst of incredible speed as he saw Liana begin the signal for the finale.

The captain brought her cutlasses above her head in an X pattern—the signal for all troops, including the archers, to pull back from the mountain. Once they got far enough, Liana brought her swords down quickly. A flaming arrow shot into the sky, the final signal that the enemy was demoralized enough.

When he saw the flaming arrow, Zeg fired one of the *Freewind*'s cannons, sending a ball of steel crashing into the ice mountain. The resulting cave-in buried the tunnel, with all the escaping soldiers within.

"So," Lunen asked Liana and Leito as he and Winnie came to a complete stop, "how many do you think we got?"

"Given the amount we heard they had, and how many bodies are out here," Leito said, "along with what was in the tunnel, I'd say we killed two-thirds of them."

"Better than Thermopolo, right Winnie?" Liana asked.

"Thermopylae," Winnie corrected Liana weakly, feeling nauseous now that the adrenaline had stopped rushing through her veins. "How do we know if they won't try again?"

"Considering how many our little forces took from them, I doubt they have the stomach to keep fighting," Lunen answered, his eyes on the damage his mountain had suffered.

"We'll know soon enough," Liana said, watching the horizon leading to a cliff that oversaw the shore where the enemy had landed. A glowing spot launched into the sky, a signal arrow that the enemy was leaving.

The Empire's greatest unit had been beaten back by simple hunters in a land with no moon. And to add to the joy, the defenders had suffered only injuries on their side, no deaths. They raised their weapons and roared their victory to the heavens.

In time, we learned that our battle in the South came to be known as the Pocket War, due both to its length and the amount of forces standing against the Imperial Army. Due to a Triblood's involvement, rumor spread that we had only won through treachery and deceit.

Liana was disappointed because our "payment" ended up being our food and weapons used during that battle. So you could say that we were paid in advance. I had never seen Liana cry before that moment of realization.

I often wondered if the Empire would try again when we left, but Lunen reassured me that Imakur's pride would cause him to chase us down instead of attacking the village, something easy to imagine now that we all bore a bounty of a thousand gold pieces a head. Lunen was ecstatic about it.

Personally, I could do with no bounty at all.

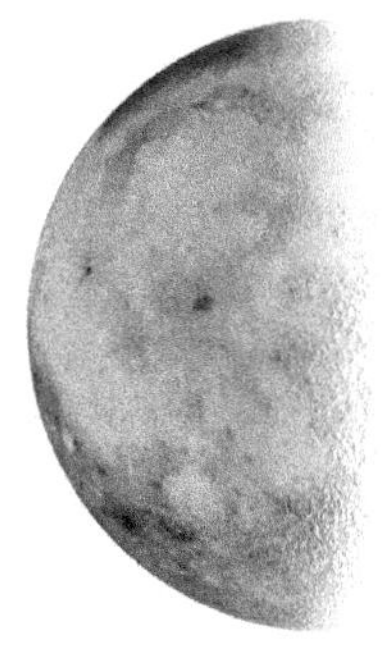

CHAPTER 4: Resistance

The world with three moons operated in its own manner. The great tribes from the mountains and deserts of the Red continent and the nobility of the Golden houses in their cities made up the upper classes. Winnie initially thought that people's innate abilities determined their class, but, as it was on her world, family seemed to dictate one's place in life more than ability.

This did not stop the Golden houses from arranging births according to lunar charts, enabling the births of children with three full Gold-moons.

The Red-mooners were less concerned with the sizes of one's moons and more with the size of one's tribe. The old saying was, "You offend one Red-mooner, be prepared for his whole family."

The Blue continent's ways were mysterious. All anyone outside knew was that the people were more spiritual than materialistic. The only currency was that of gold and silver.

But in the old days, the nations maintained a respect for each other, and the more affluent were helpful to those not born into fortune. Poverty only became a reality with the Masked Emperor. Everyone knew the story of the tyrant, if not his true name or face.

The Peacekeepers were an honored unit, their members consisting of people from both the Red and Gold lands. Their leaders were chosen from a great bloodline that cared not for the size of one's moons but their ability to lead. Their purpose was simple: to aid the different nations in times of disaster and to stop conflicts from becoming too large. They operated from a great floating castle, held aloft by gaianite. The last true leader of the Peacekeepers was blessed with only one male heir, as well as a forgotten daughter, long assumed to be dead. A decade after the boy's birth, his parents died. The boy took control of the Peacekeepers. As he grew, their name changed to the Imperial army. He then declared himself Emperor of the world.

Each nation's pride over who should lead a resistance against the Imperial army prevented their success. Eventually most of the Gold-mooners fell in line with the army, though some still resisted in border skirmishes. The Red-mooners turned their land into a constant divided battleground against the Empire, and the Blue-mooners isolated themselves from the world. The Empire levied huge taxes against any living in the territories that bowed to them, and only those of great families could avoid impoverishment. The rest of the world suffered. But in any age of oppression, there is always resistance.

Migs filled Winnie in as she walked with him and several other crew members into a bar in a dusty town in the desert hills of the Red continent. Liana and the *Freewind* crew had had more than enough dealings with the resistance group they were about to meet with. The captain would admit that the profits were always good, but the danger was often high enough for them to argue over the jobs. "I'm going to die here, aren't I?" Winnie asked.

"Only if you stray, or talk out of line to someone with more than enough strength to tear your head from your neck," Migs replied in a deadpan tone.

Winnie was not sure if she should explain that by "here," she meant dying on this world, and now that he'd said that, she felt she should keep her eyes open for anyone capable of doing severe damage to her body. *Of course, under this moon, someone half my size could probably kill me just as easily,* she thought.

Over fifty members of the crew filed into the bar and began mingling with the patrons already there. This served two purposes: it rewarded those who had done well during the recent jobs, and it provided cover for the meeting about to take place beneath the building.

Liana had begun to lead Leito, Zeg, Migs, and Lunen to a door behind the bar but paused when she saw Winnie following behind Lunen. "Exactly *why* is she here?" the captain asked them.

"Come on, Liana," Lunen said. "She's like a lost child."

"Gee, nice to be thought of so highly," Winnie muttered under her breath to no one in particular.

"What Lunen means is that she's liable to be safer with us than left up here," Leito said. The captain usually trusted Leito's opinion enough to change her mind. This was not one of those times.

"I'm only bringing you three along because you're ranking members in the crew, and I'm only bringing Lunen in case I need him to set someone on fire for me."

"And I'm only bringing her along so I have someone to talk to, especially given *who* we're talking with," Lunen added.

Liana sighed and said, "If you promise not to start a fight with him this time, then I'll let her come along."

Winnie wanted to ask exactly what was going on, but decided that, considering her luck so far, she was about to learn anyway.

The hidden room beneath the bar was large enough for any good-sized meeting. It reminded Winnie of the board rooms she'd seen her father lord over at the hospital when he had to take her as a child to work. While he was never a businessman, his abilities in his profession guaranteed that he would be heard. *Why am I thinking about him?* she wondered.

Liana sat at one end of the fairly long table with Leito at her right side and Migs on her left, with his twin sitting to his left. Lunen sat next to Leito, and Winnie took her place next to Lunen. People of various sizes and features filled the other side of the table, but Winnie felt her eyes drawn toward the man sitting at the end, staring down Liana.

He had pale skin, yet gave no impression of sickness or weakness. His eyes were an unearthly shade of blazing blue, and he wore his long black hair tied back in a ponytail. His features were without a doubt the most beautiful she had ever seen, with a thin nose, and a perfectly angled jaw. He wore a dark blue cloak, which made him look like some kind of odd monk. He was of similar height and build to Lunen, but presence was the key difference. Lunen's had a subtle presence, like a campfire that became part of the setting. Looking at this man was like watching a forest burn: there was no way a person could be in his presence and not notice him.

"Who is that?" she whispered to Lunen.

"Juushikahn, leader of the resistance," Lunen replied, not bothering to hide the disdain in his voice.

"I see you have brought someone new this meeting, Captain Liana," Juushikahn said in a deep voice that surprised Winnie. It was as if he was only moving his lips while a man three times his size spoke from behind a curtain. And yet there was a softness to his tone, like velvet, that made it seem disarming.

"Um...hi," she said. "My name is Winifred Winters, but I like to be called Winnie."

"It is a pleasure," he replied. "If you don't mind my saying so, there is something...otherworldly about you."

Winnie turned to look at Lunen, whose eyes remained fixed on Juushikahn. A thin bead of blood dripped from his lip, and Winnie realized he had been biting his lip since the resistance leader began speaking to her.

"You...you might say I'm something of a wanderer," she replied, feeling strangely conflicted about talking to Juushikahn.

"Well, I do hope you return to your home," he answered, a gentle smile forming on his lips.

"Can you please stop flirting with my subordinate?" Liana said at last. "You called us for a job, Juushikahn. What is it, and why should we do it?"

"It's an exchange job, Captain," Juushikahn said. "One of our splinter groups is en route to an emergency meeting point. You are to bring them food and medical supplies and to take a tablet from them and bring it to one of my agents, who will be waiting at this tavern for you. The pay is five thousand gold pieces."

"Not bad, Juushikahn," Liana replied with a smirk. "You actually skipped the 'good of the world' speech and got straight to the price."

"What's the tablet?" Lunen asked. Ignoring Liana's glare, he added, "And where is the meeting point?"

"Ah, Lunen," Juushikahn said, a playful tone in his voice, "You always provide the entertainment at these meetings." He finally stood up. "The tablet is a clue to the Tower."

"Not the Tower again," Liana groaned, cradling her head. "It's just a myth."

"The Tower is the single greatest prize in this world," Juushikahn said, as if reciting holy doctrine. "Once found, it will allow anyone to do anything—even travel worlds."

Did he just look at me when he said that? Winnie wondered.

"Come on, Liana. You know that nearly every delivery involves something to do with the Tower," Lunen said, a small grin on his face. "It's about the only way he'll ever make any progress on defeating the Emperor."

"Better than hiding from the conflict like you, Triblood," Juushikahn growled.

"Since when do I hide?" Lunen replied. "I deal with the Empire when they're right in front of me, instead of plotting in the shadows and sending others like you, Juushikahn."

"Sooo, where's the meeting spot?" Winnie asked, hoping to break up the fight.

"I'm glad you asked," Juushikahn said, growing weary of the argument. "It's at the Zero Point."

"No!" Lunen growled. "We're not doing it!"

"Lunen!" Liana yelled. "You do not speak for this crew!"

"Are you insane, Liana? You know that the Zero Point is too dangerous!"

"But what about the people who need supplies?" Winnie asked, for once forgoing the traditional 'What are we talking about' question.

"She's right, Lunen," Juushikahn said. "Those people need these supplies. Will your dislike of my methods condemn them?"

"My hating you has never stopped me from doing what Liana ordered," Lunen muttered under his breath.

"Then I say we take the job. It *is* five thousand gold pieces," Liana said, her tone clearly indicating that money was the last thing on her mind after Lunen's recent outburst.

"Fine," Lunen said, looking very agitated. Winnie had noticed that all of the crewmembers present had seemed shocked at his outburst, as if it was not normal for him to react so strongly.

"Are you all right?" she asked Lunen.

"Why don't you ask Mister Arrogant Leader-type?" he replied.

Juushikahn was fighting for the people. Lunen's loyalty was seemingly more immediate to the people he cared about. Juushikahn led from the shadows while Lunen stood at the foreground, in the Emperor's sights. And for the life of me, I didn't know who to side with.

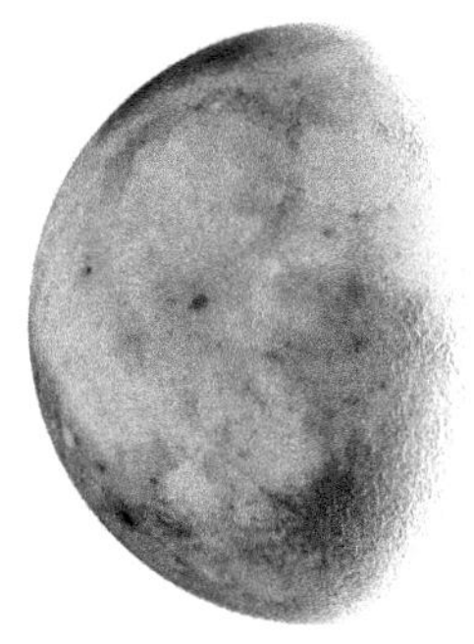

CHAPTER 5: Old Wounds

"I can't believe you!" Liana yelled at Lunen. The members of the crew that had gone to the rendezvous were making their way back to the *Freewind,* hidden in a box canyon nearby. Liana and her circle from the meeting were lagging behind so she could yell at Lunen without losing face.

"Exactly what did I do wrong?" Lunen asked.

"You lost your damn temper!" the captain screamed in anger. "I know you don't like Juushikahn's methods. I know you don't appreciate the danger we end up in doing his jobs. And I know damn well you'd love nothing more than beat him within an inch of his life and get away with it, but you not only embarrassed yourself but your captain and your crew as well!"

"When I joined this crew," Lunen growled, "I promised you that I'd support you and make sure that your dream of being as good a captain as your father would come true. And you promised that you'd never give me an order that I would hate. And yet here we are, about to commit suicide just because Juushikahn flashed some gold!"

"An order you'd hate? Lunen, in the years you've been on my ship, you've never told anyone what you'd never do! And you have done some of the most insane things I've ever seen for the fun of it. Hell, I would have thought you'd love to go to the Zero Point just to prove how strong you are!"

"You know, maybe we should just stop and relax for a few seconds, regain our composure?" Winnie asked, immediately regretting jumping in between these two.

"And you!" Liana said, turning to face Winnie. "If you had just stayed quiet, we might have been able to back out of this job. But no, you had to bring up the people needing supplies, making us look cruel if we backed down!"

"Do *not* take it out on her!" Lunen said, grabbing the captain's shoulder. The others held their breath, unsure of what would happen.

"Tell me, Lunen," Liana said quietly, not even turning to face him, "did you act as you did because of the Zero Point or because Juushikahn dared to talk to this girl who, for some insane reason, you've attached yourself to?"

Lunen removed his hand and stormed off, leaving the others behind.

"Who are you?" Liana asked Winnie. "Since Lunen joined us, he's always known when to keep it together in front a client. He's done things that most warriors would think twice about before attempting. And you show up, and he loses control? Who the hell are you, Winnie?"

"I'm just...I mean..." Winnie stopped and sighed. "I don't know how I came here, but this isn't my world. One day I just ended up here. I'm still not sure what happened. Lunen was the first friend I made here, and he seemed like the only one I could trust."

A brief silence followed as the group stared at her.

"That explains a lot," Leito said at last. "Her absolute ignorance of everything we know as fact, Juushikahn's comments to her about worlds…"

"You think he was trying to tell me the Tower would help get me home?" Winnie asked, attempted to interrupt.

"Hell, even what happened with Lunen makes some sense!" Zeg added, cutting Winnie off.

"How does *that* make any sense?" Liana asked incredulously.

"Captain, let's be honest," Migs said. "Regardless of how we have come to respect him, we all saw him first as a Triblood before anything else. Lunen *would* become attached to someone who thought of him as himself first and a Triblood second."

"And with Juushikahn blatantly telling Winnie how she could leave, that would set him off," Liana said with growing realization.

"I hate to be a pain," Winnie said carefully, "but three things I think I should say right now: Lunen did get angry when Juushikahn spoke to me, but he only snapped when the Zero Point was brought up. Secondly, why is it so easy for people to believe I'm from another world?"

"We have often heard myths and stories about creatures from different worlds beyond our own. Usually I would just think of them as fantasy," Migs said.

"Where I come from, a guy who heals so fast it's like he wasn't hurt would be nothing but fantasy," Winnie icily replied to the doctor.

"What was the third thing?" Zeg asked.

"What the hell is the Zero Point?"

The universe is built on many inherent laws, and one of the fundamental laws is that of attraction. Metaphysical discussion makes several arguments that this applies to not only gravity but the effect of thought and will on the universe. But among the greatest examples of this fundamental law are the tides.

Any world that has both a moon and water will show the attraction between the two. The tides shift and move, following the moon. What most people do not know is that the effect of the high tide under the moon is mirrored on the other side of the world. In a world with one moon, such as the one Winnie came from, this means there were two areas, each in opposite hemispheres, experiencing high tide. However, in a world with multiple moons, the effect is more drastic.

With three moons, this world had its own unique tidal system. The Red and Gold moons orbited at such a speed with the rotation of the world that they always hung above the middle of the two continents that took their names from the heavenly bodies' colors. In fact, the two moons only shifted as the position of the planet's tilted axis turned in relation to its sun. This created the phases that determined so much for the abilities of those beneath the moons. This also caused the tides to be twice as high and strong as those on the world with one moon, due to the two moons being perfectly opposite in their positions.

The Blue-moon, however, followed a bizarre elliptical orbit. It circled the Northern continent, churning the tide around it. All these tidal forces came together in the largest ocean on this world. All this came together in the very center of that ocean, at the point where the sun must pass in order for it to be a new day. On Winnie's world, this would be called the International Date Line. On this world with three moons, it was called the Zero Point.

Winnie watched as the crew loaded supplies onto the *Freewind.* "That's very interesting," she said after learning about the Zero Point, "but I don't get why it seems so feared."

"For one thing," Leito replied, "the mixing of the various tides there makes it a perpetual storm zone. Pelting rain, dangerous winds, and unstable waves make the area a death trap. The Empire has no patrols there because whether a ship is in the air or on the water, its crew is likely to die."

"The other point is that supposedly, there's a beast livin' in the waters of the storm right under the Zero Point," Zeg added. "It reaches out of the depths for any ship on the water and tears it apart and feeds on its crew, draggin' 'em into the deep."

"Wow," Winnie said. "I can't believe I got us into this."

"Well, there's no proof the creature is real," Leito said in his most reassuring voice, which only earned a snort from Zeg.

"Yeah. Cause no one's seen it and lived to talk about it."

Winnie paused as she processed this. *Irrational response, a horrible monster in the worst part of the world...*

She quickly made her way to her Triblood friend, whom she found sitting at a bench by a tavern's door. Wind-hunter sat curled near his legs.

"You've seen what's in the Zero Point, haven't you?" she asked.

"How the hell did you..."

"A guy who fights for his life as much as you do wouldn't be afraid of something unless you'd seen it before," Winnie said.

"And being afraid is the only logical reason why you would freak out like you did."

"So that's what caused such an outburst from you?" Liana said, stepping out from the neighboring market with a sack of supplies for the trip.

"Damn. This is just turning into one lousy evening," Lunen grunted. "Before my parents died, we had passed through the Zero Point. We barely made it out alive, and that was only because of my father. I'm not going through that again. Trust me, this is something you can't deal with. I still have problems thinking about it without becoming a shaking mess."

"I could deal with it, if you're there," Liana replied. "But I did promise not to make you do anything you didn't want."

Liana walked past the Triblood toward the ship. She gave Winnie a look the auburn-haired girl did not understand at first. "Since we'll have to come this way in order to drop off the item, you can wait for us here," the captain called over her shoulder to the Triblood.

Winnie could not face Lunen. She felt like she had betrayed him by causing the crew to accept this dangerous job.

"You're not going to say something like, 'I should face my fear'?" Lunen suddenly asked her.

"No," Winnie replied. "The day you met me, I was running from my own fears. Last thing I would want to be is a hypocrite."

She'd begun to slowly walk toward the ship when she felt as though something was following her. She turned, expecting the Triblood, but saw only the sky-lynx. *I guess Lunen still wants to help, even if he doesn't come along.*

"I'm surprised," Liana said as they lifted off.

As it began to rain, Winnie sat on the deck next the captain, stroking Wind-hunter's head.

"I was hoping you'd be the one to tell him how to get past his fears," Liana said.

"Fears are easier to talk about when they aren't yours," Winnie replied dejectedly.

It took hours to reach the Zero Point, and only because they pushed the *Freewind* to its absolute limits of speed, even going as far as retreating below deck to avoid being flung from the ship. After arriving, the crew finally stepped back on deck and began the arduous task of transporting supplies from the *Freewind* to the smaller resistance airship.

Winnie would have thought it comical, watching Red-mooners tossing large crates from one ship to the other like they were pillows. Of course, she was still thinking about Lunen. "I know what it's like to be so scared you want to just avoid any and everything to do with it," she told Liana as the transfer of supplies continued. "Don't know why I thought he'd be any different."

"I wouldn't write him off yet," Liana replied. "Lunen is no different from anyone. Everyone is afraid of things. Everyone suffers under his or her own grief. But, if they try, everyone can do what he does."

"Throw lightning bolts?" Winnie replied wryly.

"Do what's right," Liana quipped back. "Whether it's for himself, you, me, the crew, I've never known him to let anyone go it alone. Hell, he even lent us Wind-hunter."

"Captain!" the resistance ship's captain called out. "Ready for the tablet?"

"Sure!" Liana said, making her way to the guardrail. "Just throw it over!"

Winnie stood up, wondering how tossing a tablet in storm conditions would play out. She smiled as Liana began to move into the wind, getting ready to chase the artifact down if push came to shove. As the young resistance captain threw it into the air, presumably with Red-moon strength, Liana took off, leaping into the air to catch it. Just as her hands gripped the small, stone slab, a massive tentacle rose from the water and smashed into the side of the small resistance ship.

"It's the beast!" someone screamed, and Winnie saw everyone scrambling as more tentacles began to rise round the ship.

Wait. We're, like, a few stories above the ocean, she thought.

At that moment, a colossal form rose from the waters, towering high above the *Freewind*, its body reminiscent of the snake-like form of the gorgons Winnie read about in middle school, with the exception of its four arms instead of two. The rain and darkness obscured the details of its head, but when the lightning flashed, she could briefly make out a distinctly fish-like face.

"*That's* the thing here?" Winnie cried incredulously. She was still trying to figure out if the cylindrical body segmented into the tentacles surrounding the ship, or if they may have grown from the serpentine form like branches from a tree and trailed on until the bottom of the ocean floor.

"No wonder he didn't want to come here!" Liana yelled to her, quickly securing the tablet in a pouch strapped to her belt. As one of the gargantuan hands reached down toward the already-damaged resistance ship, the captain of the *Freewind* screamed, "Emergency rescue protocols!"

"Not to argue, Captain," Leito yelled as he swiped at a tentacle that was beginning to entwine itself around the ship with his polearm, "but I don't think we have protocols for situations like this!"

"What we need is something to keep these appendages occupied!" Migs yelled as he tossed a spear into one of the aforementioned tendrils.

"On it!" Zeg announced as he ran to the forefront with more than a little glee.

The little man only paused to wipe the rain from his goggles before reaching into his coat. He began pulling out various tubes of different colored liquids, combining them with incredible speed and pouring the final product into several metal shafts. He then produced a folding crossbow from the seemingly limitless depths of his coat.

"You carry all that around with you?" Winnie yelled as she helped the crewmen stab at an encroaching tentacle.

"Never know when you'll get a chance to play!" Zeg replied with a slightly demented grin as he quickly loaded and fired the shafts containing his new concoction at each of the creature's limbs, including the massive hand. Within moments smoke began rising from the small penetration points, and the tentacles retreated into the murky depths. The creature's gargantuan torso pulled back into the water, a strange growl emanating from its jaws.

"Odd, brother, that it did not explode like some of your usual concoctions," Migs commented with a small smirk.

"Too little time to make a good explosion, brother," Zeg replied. "Best I could do was a short-working acid. We won't have too much time."

"Then let's evacuate the resistance members onto our ship before theirs crashes!" Liana commanded.

The crew worked quickly, tossing cables to bring the dying ship closer. Surviving resistance members tried leaping the shortened distance or swinging from ropes tied to their own masts. Winnie finally took a moment to remove her glasses, as the rainfall had made them more of a hindrance than a help, and saw Wind-hunter pacing around the *Freewind*'s center mast. He attempted to take off, but the combination of wind and rain made his wings useless.

"We've almost got them all off! As soon as the last one is on board, we rise," Liana ordered. "I'd rather take my chances in the storm clouds than this close to the water!"

Before the last resistance member could make the leap, however, a tentacle smashed straight through the hull of his ship from below. As he tumbled to the depths, more tentacles rose, taking turns slamming into the *Freewind.* While the ship had been built to take abuse, there was no telling how long they could last.

Wind-hunter attempted to leap at one tentacle and was batted aside and into the ocean as the serpent-like body rose once more from the depths.

"Wind-hunter!" Winnie yelled. Without thinking about it, she tied a rope to her waist. "I'm going in!"

"Leito, get ready to pull her out! Migs, secure the line to the mast!" Liana commanded in response.

"Winnie, catch!" Zeg cried out as he tossed a pair of goggles to her.

Securing the goggles to her head, Winnie dived over the guardrail. As she fell, she tried to rationalize why she was even doing this. All she could think of was that she did not want the poor animal to die. She shut her eyes as she pierced the waves. When she opened them, she saw the poor creature sinking fast into the depths. She began pushing her body, trying to ignore the burning in her lungs. As soon as she managed to wrap her arms around the sky-lynx, she finally looked and saw what was truly below the surface.

The ocean floor seemed to glow as thousands of blue eyes with hourglass-shaped pupils gazed up at her. But there were no faces, just a mass of tentacles, writhing and shifting, possibly causing the unstable waves—and those eyes covered those tentacles. The creature's body went on for miles, illogical and chaotic. As Winnie gazed at one massive tentacle rising from the center, with the horrific realization that she was staring at the shaft attached to the main torso, Winnie screamed with mind-numbing terror and tugged fiercely at the rope. Thankfully, she was hoisted out of the water quickly.

"Winnie! Winnie!"

What?

"Come on, you idiot. Talk to me!"

Liana? "What happened?" Winnie said at last, coughing weakly.

"You passed out," Liana answered, sitting on the ground with her hands still gripping Winnie's shoulders. "Amazingly, you still kept a grip on the sky-lynx."

"I get it now," Winnie said weakly, only dimly aware of the continuing struggle between the airship and the monstrosity that had them surrounded from below. "It can't be beaten. He knew that."

"You're making less sense than usual, Winnie, and that's starting to scare me."

"No wonder he seemed so hurt…I condemned us all…"

"Winnie," Liana growled, dragging the girl to her feet, "with our luck, we would have ended up here at some point anyway. Now either get up and fight, or I'll throw you back overboard."

"It's the same thing!" Winnie shrieked, surprising both the captain and herself. "No one can beat that thing! We're going to die!"

"Captain, we got company!" a voice called from the central mast.

"What?" Liana said, dragging Winnie with her.

"You feel that?" Winnie asked.

"I don't feel anything," Liana said.

"Exactly."

The pounding and pulling from the tentacles had stopped. The serpentine figure still stood monolithic against the dark sky. The rain continued to pound down on them, and lightning continued to flash, but the creature stood completely still, seeming to gaze in the direction the crew could now see another ship coming from.

Winnie thought it must be about the size of a tank, and the design was almost predatory in nature. The vessel was shaped like a large box, its front seemingly filed and sharpened to look like a bird's beak. As it streaked across the sky toward them, they all knew from experience it was gunmetal grey. This was one of the Empire's small squad transports.

"Damn! Why would an Imperial squad come here?" Liana asked under her breath.

"Since Lunen isn't here to answer me, why did it stop attacking?" Winnie asked in response.

"I heard that animals are instinctually afraid of Blue-mooners, since they're not used to things that inherently alter the laws of nature," Liana said.

"Doesn't the Empire have only one Blue-mooner working for them?"

The two women felt a lump in their throats at the prospect of facing Imakur again while out in that storm-cursed area.

"Captain?" Winnie began slowly, "do we really want to see what that thing does when it's afraid?"

They both felt the lump get larger.

The tension in the air thickened as the Imperial ship came closer. With an earsplitting roar, the creature attacked it, a mass of tendrils rising from the water. It ensnared the small vessel in an instant and began to crush the metal frame.

The cockpit of the ship exploded outward, and a very human figure soared through the air toward the *Freewind.* As he came closer, the crew could see the light of electricity begin to crackle in his arms, illuminating his face.

"*Lunen?*" multiple voices cried out.

A bolt of lightning fired from his outstretched hands, striking the beast in its chest. As he began to fall, the Triblood managed to say one thing: "*Help!*"

Winnie jumped over the guardrail again, hoping the rope around her waist would still hold. *Why am I jumping back in?*

She saw the horror again as soon as she hit the water, but this time she saw Lunen facing the mass of eyes, his hands again outstretched. A massive spear of ice formed from the water in a straight path between the Triblood and the central torso-tendril. As it punctured the beast's main body, Winnie grabbed Lunen and began to pull at the rope.

As Leito pulled them back up and they broke the surface, Lunen broke the silence.

"You look better in glasses."

Winnie quickly pulled off the goggles and stared at him. "How are you so damn *calm*? I thought you were terrified of this thing?"

"Winnie, I'm dangerously close to passing out from my heart pounding so fast. Just enjoy the damn joke," he growled.

As they were hoisted over the guardrail, Liana gave Lunen a very pointed glare. Lunen tried to give his usual grin in response, but the best he could manage was a very weak smile.

"So the Imperial ship?" Liana asked.

"Took me an hour to find a group of soldiers to steal it from," Lunen replied.

"How'd you learn to fly it?"

"I know a lot of submission holds?"

"Lunen, you're sounding rather meek for...well, you."

"After seeing this thing again, I realize my memories didn't do it justice for how scary it is."

Liana sighed and then placed her hand on his shoulder. "Well, the important thing is that you came."

Lunen smiled as Winnie helped him to his feet, and Leito, Migs, and Zeg clapped him on the back.

"So, Captain, wanna give this thing a taste o' the ol' spark-out?" Zeg asked.

"Let's do it," Liana replied.

"Gonna need time to get the bits," the small engineer added.

"Time is only bought with action, people," Liana yelled. "So get to it!"

Zeg grinned and quickly dashed to the ship's hold. Lunen watched as the creature began to reach down into the water, trying with all four of its arms to remove the massive weapon of ice from its body.

The tentacles rose back up from the depths, attempting to ensnare the airship. The Triblood slammed his fist into the deck, and a strange ripple passed across the rainwater. After the familiar sound of water solidifying into ice in moments, the tentacles pulled back, blood streaming from fresh wounds. Winnie quickly dashed to the guardrail, gazing over to see what had occurred. Lunen had caused the water along the sides and bottom of the *Freewind* to stretch out and freeze, creating a porcupine-like shield of icicles.

"Water! The second easiest thing to manipulate for a Bluemooner!" Lunen yelled to her over the rain, his bravado doing its best to hold back his natural fear of the appendages.

It was then that Zeg returned, brandishing a pair of six-foot-long metal poles, one with a spearhead at its tip. As Zeg and his twin hurriedly attached the two pieces, Lunen and Leito rushed to the ship's bow. The creature had finally freed itself of Lunen's ice-spear, and its massive torso leaned forward, its huge hands about to smash into the ship.

Leito leapt at the closest massive fist, stabbing his halberd between its knuckles before pushing off and landing back on the deck. As Lunen brought his hands out as far as they could stretch away from each other, balls of water rose off the deck. He tightened his fists, and they stretched into flat, frozen discs. He pivoted on the balls of his feet, and as his hands passed the point between him and the second encroaching giant hand, a disc launched. The second appendage reeled as chunks of ice poked out from injured, scaled flesh.

The creature's two remaining hands slammed into the bottom of the ship, ignoring the icy armor. The *Freewind* suddenly lurched upward, sending crewmembers stumbling, falling, or flying. Liana was of the latter and went over the edge of the guardrail. Her fingers reached out in desperation—and closed around thura bone.

Winnie pulled back as hard as she could. While Liana was smaller than her, it did not change the fact that rain had made both her staff and the guardrail she'd propped her foot on slick. With all her strength, she managed to pull the captain back on board.

"You guys ready with that?" Lunen asked pointedly to the ship's resident geniuses.

"Winnie, with me!" Liana ordered as she rushed to grab the front of the new spear. Winnie quickly picked up the lower half, and the two rushed toward the front of the airship. For the briefest moment, Liana thought that the run from the center of the deck to the bow seemed to blur and become shorter.

As Liana and Winnie approached, Leito reached behind him and gripped the massive spear, raising it above his head. As the monster rushed forward, its massive jaws opening with all intent to crush the ship in its mandibles, the first mate threw his weapon straight at the beast's forehead with all his Red-moon strength. As it pierced its target, Lunen raised his left hand to the heavens and aimed his right at the beast. A bolt of lightning shot down from the clouds, striking the Triblood and traveling through his body, blasting out of his outstretched hand and striking the spear. An ear-shattering roar filled the air, followed by a titanic splash as the beast fell to the depths.

"You just carry a twelve-foot spear on board?" Winnie cried in what was becoming her most familiar voice.

Lunen coughed a small amount of smoke, and fell onto his back, mumbling, "Can we please take the damn tablet back now?"

"Lunen, you just took a lightning bolt while we were in the rain, and we are all still alive. I am impressed with your control," Migs said with a smirk.

"Y'know, I just realized," Zeg chuckled, "this whole thing explains why Lunen disappears when we buy food that has tentacles."

Liana laughed and said, "Everyone, save whatever tentacles you find. We're going to make Lunen shriek like a little girl!"

"I hate you all," Lunen groaned.

As Liana delivered both the resistance survivors and the tablet to Juushikahn, Winnie and Lunen stayed behind on the ship. An awkward silence passed between them as they both watched the rising sun after the long trip back.

"I'm sorry," Winnie said. "If I'd bothered just listening, we wouldn't have had to deal with that."

"It's all right," Lunen replied quietly. "If anything, I finally had a chance to settle it with that thing. I'm still going to have nightmares about it until I die, but at least I faced it."

"Why did you come back?"

"I asked myself if it was worth losing everyone I care about just to not face something I was afraid of."

"I wish it was that easy for me to face what scared me." She sighed.

"Well, look at it this way," he said as he put his hand on her shoulder, "you're not alone. And whatever happens, we'll all face it together—even if it's the beast at the Zero Point again."

"Again?" she asked as she pulled back slowly.

"Yeah. It's immortal," he said casually.

"I hate this world," she groaned.

While I still found myself nursing a crush on the resistance leader, I'd learned that just jumping into trouble for that infatuation wasn't always smart. Still, it felt good finally knowing I could trust Liana and the crew, that they were as much my friends as Lunen was.

I realized that my question to Lunen about him coming back was pointless. Like Liana had tried to tell me, he did what he thought was right, on his terms and no one else's. And after all, I saw what that monster was and I still dived in after the crazy Triblood anyway. It made sense in a strange way. I too would rather see something horrific again if it meant helping someone I cared about.

At the back of my mind, I felt a growing fear that fighting the creature in the Zero Point was not going to be a one-time event for me. But I knew that if we had to face it again, we'd do it as a crew.

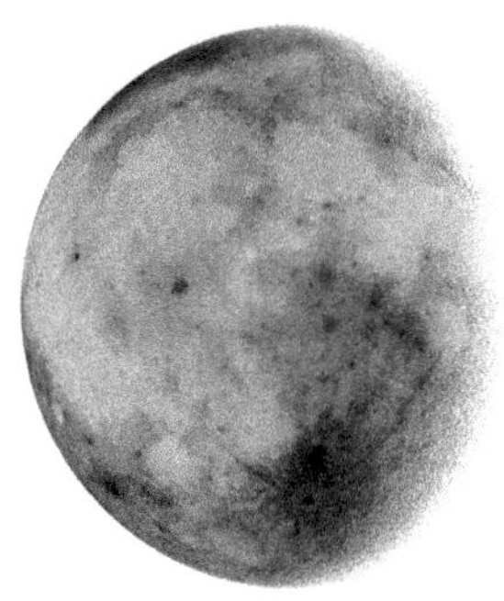

CHAPTER 6:
To Be Strong

Winnie grumbled to herself as she awoke, her hands blindly reaching for her glasses. She was starting to worry about the fact that waking up so early had become a habit by this point. After the battle in the South, Leito had taken to waking her up early so he could train her on the *Freewind*'s deck. A week had passed since the encounter at the Zero Point, and Winnie was not looking forward to another session of staff spins and duck-and-roll exercises. She quickly dressed in the loose pants and almost-tank-top Liana had lent her and made her way out of the captain's quarters.

She'd been as stunned as anyone when Liana asked if she wanted to stay in her room. Apparently, since the discovery of Winnie's otherworldly origins, Liana felt it would be better for Winnie to stay with the only other female on the ship so as to not be taken advantage of, instead of sleeping on the deck next to Lunen. Lunen had commented that it was probably a way to make up for snapping at Winnie and not taking her seriously until the battle at the Zero Point, an idea Liana vehemently denied.

Is this what I've been missing out on? Winnie wondered as she picked up her thura-bone staff. As she made her way to the deck, she reflected on how she often avoided socializing with people, being completely ostracized in high school and only connecting with her roommate in college. Maybe if she had stopped worrying about pleasing her father, she could have gone out clubbing when Jennifer invited her.

Jennifer…God, I hope she isn't worrying herself to death over me.

Winnie's thoughts screeched to a grinding halt when she noticed that Leito was nowhere to be seen and that a certain Triblood stood waiting where the first mate normally stood.

"Morning!" Lunen greeted cheerfully.

"Um…where's Leito? We were going to do more training," Winnie said, worrying just where this was going to lead.

"Leito won't be training you for a while," Lunen answered. "Apparently, he's very impressed by you. He says that you have a natural gift for reading body language, dodging, and using your weapon."

"You mean that I'm good enough to take care of myself now?" Winnie asked, her self-esteem starting to swell.

"Of course not," Lunen said, dropping the smile. "You're still pitifully inexperienced, especially in dealing with people from the various moons here, and you lack both commitment and understanding of strategy. That's why Leito asked me to take over training you."

"Wait…I mean, that's not completely true," Winnie said, already letting the criticism affect her newly raised confidence.

"Can you beat me?" Lunen asked plainly.

"No..." Winnie answered dejectedly.

"Wrong," Lunen replied. "I'm not invincible. No one is. Anyone can be defeated. Likewise, anyone can win. The only reason you say you can't beat me is because you don't know how yet, and you sell yourself short. I'm going to change that."

"Lunen, I can't beat people who were born stronger than me."

"Why not? I made it this far with only a bare-bones understanding of fighting techniques. And you did good during our fight down south."

"You were keeping an eye on me; that's why."

"Winnie, no battle, physical or otherwise, can be won if you don't know that you *can* win." Lunen gave her a wicked grin. "I'm going to make your will strong..."

Three hours had passed, and Winnie felt worse than in any of her training sessions with Leito. As she fell backward onto the deck from exhaustion, Lunen sat down next to her, his legs crossed, beaming.

"You're learning to use those elbow strikes good, and your legwork is impressive for your first day. And damn, Leito was right about your skill in dodging. I'd swear you had Red-moon speed with the way you got out of the way," Lunen said, beaming with what Winnie imagined was a sadistic sense of pride.

"Lunen, I'm not strong," she said quickly, as her breathing had become shallow with fatigue. "I'm lucky I can lift the staff half the time. I can't break things, or knock people out with a single blow..."

"That isn't strength," Lunen said, his voice suddenly taking on a more serious tone. "Those kinds of things are incidental. True strength is measured by only one thing."

Winnie rolled off her back to her side, finally facing Lunen. "What's that?"

"What you can protect," Lunen answered solemnly, as if reciting religious doctrine. "My parents always told me that the first measure of strength was being able to protect yourself. That included your beliefs, your opinions, and your principles. If you continued to get stronger, you could protect those who were around you all the time. In time, you could protect those who were rarely around you, and if you could achieve that level of strength, you could eventually protect everything you ever wanted to."

Winnie watched his face as he spoke, noting a familiar, quiet sadness she had not seen since he'd told her about his parents. She could not imagine what failing to protect family meant to someone who measured strength in such a way.

"OK. Lesson's over," Lunen said, quickly brightening up. "If I remember, today is Leito and your turn to cook, so here's hoping breakfast is delicious!"

"I had my first training session with Lunen," Winnie said. She intended her tone to sound icy, but her exhaustion made it sound pitiful.

"Sounds like you got some good exercise," Leito chuckled, placing a large amount of vegetables in front of her to chop before he began carving a large slab of leftover thura meat. The kitchen of the *Freewind* was the most claustrophobic area of the ship, with barely enough room for two people to work around the cutting station, the massive pot with a tube feeding heat from the engine room, various storage units filled with food, and the large oven and stove, also heated by the engine's power. It took Winnie a few cooking sessions to get used to it. Now, she just focused on chopping vegetables.

"He's got a really deep idea of strength, but I still don't see why he has to train me," Winnie commented, stifling a yawn.

"Because I'm not qualified to teach you what you need if you're going to have to fight with no one to aid you," Leito said, stifling a yawn of his own while stripping a long strand of meat from bone before tossing it into the bubbling pot. "Girl, don't yawn in front of me. One person yawns, someone else just has to yawn."

Winnie chose to ignore the yawn discussion and focus on the real issue. "Just how are you not qualified to teach me?"

"Because I'm a Red-mooner," Leito replied. "I have only two full Red-moons and one Red half-moon in me. All my tactics and knowledge focus on using that aspect of me. Liana has only one full Red-moon in her, and she learned to fight using that. The twins are both filled with three full Gold-moons. They learned how to fight with that in them. None of us could tell you how to fight someone much more powerful than you, or one who can recover quickly from your attacks, because none of us knows what it's like to be that outmatched. And *none* of us have any idea what to do when faced with a Blue-mooner. Lunen is a Triblood, constantly the one you wouldn't bet on, but in ten years in the arena and six years with us, he has fought and beaten people who had more than he did."

"Wait, you mean that…" Winnie started to say.

"Yes," Leito said. "If there was anyone who could teach someone with no moon not only how to get back up after being knocked down but how to bring down different fighters on this world, it'd be him."

"If he's so strong," Winnie asked, dropping the chopped vegetables into the pot, "why doesn't he fight the Emperor?"

"Juushikahn's rubbing off on you," Leito muttered, adding the meat carvings after her. "Despite the attitude he gives off, Lunen never really looks for a fight, only waits for one. I'm sure that, with enough time, the Emperor will come to Lunen. Only I wouldn't bet much on Lunen's chances if he doesn't develop more skill to go with all that heart."

The scent of burnt meat and garbage filled the evening air as two figures worked their way through the crowds of the Red-moon town's market. The dark and hooded robes they wore were the only thing they had in common as far as appearances go. The shorter of the two carried a polished staff made of bone, while the taller had folded his arms into the robe. As the taller one led the way, the shorter one began to cough.

"I'm going to choke on all the fumes before I learn anything," Winnie muttered, adjusting the hood. They had docked at one of the *Freewind*'s more frequent stops, and Lunen had offered to give her real fight experience in the nearby town.

"Less coughing, more talking," Lunen said. "Review: what are the greatest weaknesses of a Gold-mooner?"

"Cut off the head, pierce the brain, or completely destroy a major organ and they die," Winnie repeated from memory, struggling to keep up. "Cuts, bruises, and broken bones can heal on their own, but dislocated parts have to be placed back in; otherwise, they can't heal. Put something through the flesh and leave it, like a blade or broken bone, and the wound will not be able to close. Broken bones need to be set in order to heal properly. I think that's all of it."

"You forgot," Lunen replied with a grin, "that while some poisons are ineffective against a Gold-mooner, some are made that can overload one's healing ability, causing a long and painful death as their body tries to fight it off."

"So what would happen if someone with no healing ability got some of that poison in them?" Winnie asked as she paused to drink from her canteen.

"Instant painful death," Lunen answered, finally stopping at the entrance to an alley. "Usually Gold-mooners are the only ones to use those kinds of poisons, since they're the only ones who may live long enough to use the antidote."

"What do I do if I fight a Blue-mooner?"

"Pray that you're faster on the attack than he is," Lunen said, leading the way into the alley.

"That's it?" Winnie asked, jogging after him. "There are no little tricks or secrets you can share?"

"If you want, I can throw waves of fire at you later. Right now, I'm going to teach you something about Red-mooners."

Lunen finally stopped walking. Winnie caught up and saw why.

Three tall, muscled men were shoving a very small girl back and forth between them. Judging from the men's bronze skin tones and black hair, Winnie thought they were likely from the areas of the Red continent where the jagged mountains met the desert. The girl looked to be about her age but was incredibly petite, making it easy to initially mistake her for a much younger girl. She wore a long, pink set of clothing that could be both a robe and a dress, and her jet-black hair was tied in a ponytail. Her features were what Winnie would identify as Asian, a sign of a person of Gold lineage, and while her face was average, something in her sad eyes seemed to draw attention, as if she was someone a person could not help but want to save.

"Did you actually know about this?" Winnie whispered to Lunen.

"No," the Triblood replied, "but I knew if I walked down the right alley, I'd find someone I could demonstrate on without feeling guilty."

Never looks for a fight my ass! she thought, certain her face wore a sour expression as he walked toward the commotion.

"Excuse me, sir!" Lunen called, walking casually up to the largest of the three. "May I ask what your moons are?"

"Little man," the large one growled, holding the girl in place, "if you want to still walk away from here, you better do it now."

"Well, you see, there's a personal matter involved here," Lunen said, sliding up to the large one's side. He gave the girl a look, like he was assessing her. "Very good taste you have, my friend. I too have a thing for the ladies. In fact," he added, pointing a thumb at Winnie, "this girl bet me a night of passion if I could break a Red-mooner's hand without touching him."

Winnie's face went bright red, and when she saw that the girl was looking at her as if she was crazy, she started shaking her head rapidly.

"What do I get out of it?" the large one asked.

"The satisfaction of causing me harm without any consequence if I'm wrong?" Lunen asked innocently.

The Red-mooner laughed, and as he shoved the girl to the next largest of them, he said, "I have two full Red-moons in my blood, like my friends here."

"That would be most satisfactory." Lunen smiled, standing back against the alley's wall. "Throw me your best punch."

Winnie watched as the large one's body went through the familiar motions of a full-strength punch. As she saw the shift in weight so that his hip moved forward, adding momentum to his shoulder's own force, she realized what Leito meant by her being skilled at reading body language. As the large man's fist sailed through the air at incredible speed, Lunen sidestepped. The Triblood quickly backpedaled to Winnie as the Red-mooner's fist shattered a considerable amount of the wall. As he pulled his fist back, the large one started wailing as bone jutted through the back of his hand, blood running off his fist.

"You see, Winnie," Lunen said as he turned his head to her, "a Red-mooner's power is in the muscles, which can be trained to be even stronger, but his bones and skin are still vulnerable to damage from his own strength if they haven't been conditioned."

As he finished, Lunen was suddenly kicked in the side of his face by two boots as the smallest of the three rushed him. As the Triblood sailed through the air down the alley, the assailant quickly gripped Winnie by the throat, slamming her against the wall. As she dropped her staff to attempt to pry his fingers from her windpipe, Winnie struggled to remember what Lunen had showed her during the torture session he called training.

Her right arm crossed over his outstretched limb, her elbow coming down on his forearm, breaking his grip. Before he could react, she swung her right hand in a hammer-fist, smashing him across his face. As he stumbled backward, Winnie quickly brought her hands to the sides of her head and darted toward him, swinging her elbow in a horizontal blow against his cheek. He fell backward to the ground, and Winnie quickly retrieved her staff and brought her foot against his chest, bringing her weapon around to a defensive position against the last one standing. She was stunned that only ten seconds had passed since Lunen was kicked in the head.

Since when was I actually good at something physical? She thought.

A coughing sound came from behind her, and she glanced over her shoulder at Lunen. He was slowly walking back to them, his jaw hanging limply. Winnie realized with growing nausea that it was dislocated. When he finally reached her side, he popped it back in. If he had not screamed in agony at the act, she would have just from imagining the pain he was in.

"Damn it!" he roared. "I hate dislocations! They hurt like hell when they pop out, and they hurt just as bad when they pop in. And the fact that it heals perfectly after being popped back in just means it'll hurt just as much as the first time if it happens again!" He quickly brought his hand up, a ball of fire floating in front of his palm. As the three stared, dumbstruck, he just growled, "Yes, I'm a Triblood. Now get the hell out of here and leave the girl before I do something I'm going to really enjoy."

Winnie nearly fell as the man beneath her feet rolled out from under her and ran. The one holding the girl shoved her toward Lunen and Winnie as he quickly ran to the one with the broken hand, and then the alley was empty except for three.

"Are you OK?" Winnie asked, realizing how stupid it sounded after what she'd seen.

"At least I didn't throw up," Lunen moaned, rubbing his jaw. "Hurt so damn bad, my stomach nearly emptied. At least you did good tonight."

"I did, didn't I?" Winnie mumbled, still in awe that she'd managed to do something during a situation she'd always imagined would end horrifically for her.

The two of them then became painfully aware of the girl staring at them. She quickly bowed, avoiding their eyes.

"You can look us in the eyes, y'know," Lunen said.

"Yeah. We won't hurt you," Winnie said. "What's your name?"

"My name is Disana," the girl answered. "My moons are three full Gold, and I was abandoned as a child. I was eventually taken as a slave and sold to a brothel here in this area. I ran away, and those thugs attacked me. I owe you my life."

"More like we're responsible for it," Lunen said. When he saw Winnie's look of confusion, he continued. "She's a full Gold-mooner girl with no family ties. Brothels love using girls like that since they can't catch any diseases and no one will look for them. If we leave her here, God knows where she'll end up."

"You think Liana will let her on the crew?" Winnie asked.

"Depends," was all he said before turning back to the newcomer. "What can you do?"

"I could service your crew, if that's what you want," Disana said quietly, staring at the ground.

"*No!*" both Lunen and Winnie shouted. They looked at each other.

"Did we just shout at the same time?" Winnie asked.

"Let's not tell anyone about that," Lunen replied.

"I'm sure we can find a job for you on our ship," Winnie said. "And no one will ever use you like that again. I promise."

"You truly mean it?" Disana asked, a smile breaking across her face.

When both Lunen and Winnie nodded, she laughed and leapt into Lunen's arms. Before he could react, she kissed him on the lips. And before Winnie could react, Disana turned and kissed her in the same manner. She then ran to gather her belongings from the ground.

"Did she just..." Winnie mumbled under her breath.

"I say nothing, you say nothing," Lunen stated, the look of disbelief seemingly etched onto his face.

"So…" Liana said, looking at the new addition, "what exactly does she do?"

"Well…" Winnie started, "she's… friendly."

"Understatement of the year," Lunen said under his breath.

"If you want, I could always take care of your crew," Disana said softly.

"She means cook!" Lunen said rapidly.

"And clean!" Winnie added.

"And exactly why should I hire someone to do that when I have you two?" Liana asked, cocking her eyebrow.

"Because three gets the job done faster than two?" Lunen said cautiously.

"Come on, Captain; she's got nowhere else to go," Winnie pleaded.

Liana stared at both of them before finally sighing. "OK. Fine. She works under you two. I swear, I don't know how my ship became a halfway house."

"You have a heart of gold, Captain!" Winnie called over her shoulder as she and Lunen led Disana out of Liana's quarters.

"If only, just so I could sell it!" Liana yelled back.

"What is she doing here again?" Lunen asked, pinching the bridge of his nose.

"I don't know how she does it; she just wakes up when I do," Winnie answered, stifling a yawn.

"I had to be a light sleeper back in the brothel," Disana added in a voice far too chipper for both Lunen and Winnie's tastes.

"Disana, we spoke about this. No more 'back in the brothel' stories, OK?" Lunen grumbled.

It had been a week since the strange girl joined the *Freewind*'s crew. Disana had become popular among the various crewmembers. Some said it was because of how sweetly innocent she was—a fact that Winnie and Lunen, who kept the girl's past a secret, found rather ironic. Others said it was because of how quickly she seemed to learn things. While Winnie was still struggling with the various tasks of tying off the sails and cooking some of the dishes she'd never heard of before, Disana was already leaps and bounds ahead of her. She was also proving to be a very capable assistant to the twins in their different areas of expertise.

One aspect of her that many found odd was her doting nature toward the Triblood and Winnie. Every morning that Winnie woke up for training with Lunen, Disana followed. Whenever Lunen and Winnie left the ship during a delivery, she tagged along. It was starting to grate on Lunen's nerves.

"Seriously, how are we this likeable?" Lunen asked as he grappled Winnie from behind. He was finally bringing Winnie to better levels of self-defense, and it showed. She elbowed him in the ribs while bringing her head back sharply into his skull.

"I think we're the first nice people she's ever met. Given what happened to her, it makes a crazy kind of sense. Traumatized people tend to cling to whoever seems to cares for them."

"Why don't you care that you hurt me?" Lunen whimpered from where he'd collapsed after her head-butt.

"Well, I know you're not going to take it personally," Winnie replied, giving him a playful smile as she reached for his hand. She then gave a small yelp as he swept her legs.

"Never think for a second that anyone you fight is going to be nice about it," Lunen quipped, attempting to stand up.

"Good to know!" Winnie shouted as she kicked him in the groin.

Curling into a ball, he groaned, "Training is over for today..."

"It's so nice, the way you two are," Disana said from the spot where she sat on the side. "Most couples I serviced never seemed happy with each other."

"No more stories!" Lunen screamed.

"We are not a couple!" Winnie added.

"Aww...you two are so cute together. That's partly why I love you both so much."

"Now, Disana," Winnie said, chuckling nervously, "when you say *love...*"

"I'm in love with you both," Disana said with a smile.

"I'm going to see Migs," Lunen said as he limped away.

"But you heal fast!" Winnie exclaimed.

"I *really* don't want to have this conversation," he said quietly as he quickly made his escape.

"Damn you, Lunen!" Winnie screamed.

"You really care for him, don't you?" Disana asked as she stood up.

"For some reason, despite his moments of idiocy," Winnie said, "I mean, he *was* the first person to just want to accept me for who I wanted to be, not what he wanted."

"I know that feeling," Disana said, walking up to Winnie. "The first person I truly loved was the one who helped me leave the brothel. If it weren't for him, I'd never have thought of myself as anything more than what they wanted me to be."

"Not exactly what happened with me..." Winnie said under her breath, "but I guess that makes sense."

A moment of awkward silence passed as the two women stared at each other.

"I'm not interested in women," Winnie stated.

"Aww... Do you think Lunen..."

"No."

"Not even if I..."

"You even *try* to sleep with him, I'll strand you at the next port."

Disana smiled. "I think you *do* more than just care about him."

"Shut up," Winnie growled as she walked away. *How the hell do I end up in situations that make talking to Dad seem easy?* She wondered.

Winnie still could not believe she had reacted like a jealous rival in a romantic drama. As she curled up under the covers on the couch in the captain's quarters, she felt her brain mixing Lunen's lessons about how distance and timing are among the most important things to understanding in dealing with attacks with the image of Disana kissing him. She spent the rest of the day placing herself between Lunen and Disana at every chance she got. While Lunen seemed as sympathetic as Winnie to the girl's plight, he still felt uncomfortable with her forwardness in her experiences. But that did not change that Winnie was sure Lunen's caring nature would end up working with Disana's forwardness and finally lead to something she was hoping would never happen. Still, she still wasn't sure why the idea of them doing anything bothered her so much.

I am not jealous. Not of some emotionally disturbed, clingy little nympho, and especially not over Lunen!

Winnie realized she was trying far too hard to convince herself, and she wondered what she could do about it. If she were back home, she could have at least talked to Jennifer about it. Then she remembered she was sharing a room with another female. *A girl who could lift me over her head and toss me overboard if she felt like it.*

"Liana?"

"What, Winnie?" the captain's voice grumbled from her bed.

"Can I talk to you?"

"You're talking to me right *now,*" came the irritated response, "while I'm trying to *sleep.*"

"I just…need to talk about something,"

"Winnie, I swear to God, I will throw you overboard if there is no point to all this."

"How easy is it to seduce Lunen?"

Winnie heard a sound in the darkness, like a muffled choking.

"You all right, Captain?"

"Why the hell would I know *that*?"

"What? Oh, God. I wasn't…I'm so sorry."

"Do I want to know? Honestly, is this the kind of discussion I want to have lingering in my dreams?"

"I just…I think…" Finally, Winnie decided to swallow her pride and get to the point. "I think Disana has her eye on Lunen, and I just want to know how likely it is that she will succeed."

"Are you kidding?" Liana asked, trying hard to contain her laughter. "If I didn't know him better, I'd say he's the same as any guy who gets an itch. But I asked him why he was never chasing girls once, when he stayed on board instead of hitting the town we were at."

"What did he say?"

"He made a lot of excuses, and I finally asked him if he's ever been with a woman. That is the only time I've ever seen him blush."

"Are you kidding?"

"His social skills are rather limited to being friends or fighting with people. I doubt he's even kissed a woman."

Winnie covered her mouth to stop herself from laughing loud enough to wake any crewmembers who were still asleep. *Lunen got his first kiss at random?* That kind of information was just too much to pass up.

"Believe me, getting Lunen to do anything he's uncomfortable with will just result in the other person wasting their time."

"I see…"

"Is there a reason you're so concerned?" Liana asked, the smile evident in her voice.

"There's no reason. I was just wondering!"

"Of course you were."

"I hate you," Winnie said.

"Aww. I'm on the same level of appreciation as Lunen."

"What?"

"Winnie, you say that to him at least once every two days."

"Shut up!"

"I'm sorry. Did you just give me an order?"

"Sorry, Captain!"

Liana just kept laughing about it, and, despite her embarrassment, Winnie laughed too. It had been too long since she'd connected with someone like this, and she always found it easier to laugh like this with other women.

A loud scream suddenly interrupted their laughter, and both women grabbed their weapons and rushed to the main deck.

They found a crowd forming by the helm, and Winnie felt her heart jump as she remembered that Lunen was on duty to pilot the ship that night. As she followed the path Liana made through the crewmen, she saw Leito had taken the helm while Migs crouched, examining a figure on the floor. Wind-hunter nudged the figure constantly with his head. The man's skin was flushed, and veins strained over frozen muscles. He stared from wide-open, bloodshot eyes as his arm kept groping at thin air. *Oh. My God. It's Lunen! It can't be Lunen. Lunen can't be dying…*

"What happened?" Liana commanded.

"I'm not sure, Captain," Disana sobbed. Winnie realized with a knot forming in her stomach that Lunen was reaching toward the petite Gold-mooner. "I came to speak to him as he manned the helm, and then he gripped his neck and screamed."

"Here, Captain," Migs said, producing a small dart that he held with a handkerchief. "Be careful. I suspect it is a Gold-killer. And it looks like a long-distance dart as well."

"There could be an Imperial ship in the area, Captain," Leito said. "Some of their less-physical soldiers are trained to use long-distance assassination weapons like that."

"It'd be a beauty if it weren't just a killin' tool," Zeg added, his gaze fixed on Lunen.

"How long do you think he has?" Winnie asked at last. She looked again at the gripping motion the Triblood kept making, the knot shrinking inside her as both realization and determination grew.

"I would say three, possibly five hours, depending on how stubbornly he fights it," Migs replied, feeling Lunen's pulse. "But the agony will be unbearable."

"I think there may be a few Hestalkus trees in this area," Disana said. "I remember seeing some as we were flying this way."

"Hestalkus does tend to grow in Red-moon mountains," Leito agreed.

"And they are a key ingredient in most antitoxins," Migs added.

"If there's an Imperial squad in this area that can strike at us from so far, sending a large group out would be suicide," the captain said.

"Send me then," Winnie said.

A frightening silence followed.

Can't blame them, can I? Winnie thought.

"Winnie, you do realize how insane that is, right?" Liana asked carefully.

"Lunen would do the same for me," replied Winnie.

Liana groaned before finally saying, "Fine, but take Disana with you. Not only does she know what you're looking for, but, to be honest, she's the only person on this ship stationed under your command."

"Here, Missy," Zeg said, reaching into his coat before producing a tube with a cord attached. "If there's trouble, just yank the cord. The flare will let us know."

"Why don't I get one?" sniffed Disana.

"Because I outrank you," Winnie replied, hoping her answer sounded as gruff as she wanted. Deep down, she suspected she sounded silly.

In the light of the Red-moon, Winnie could not help but be impressed. It washed the rocky ground in crimson light, and as the moon hid behind the peaks of the mountains, the shadows made the cliff Disana led her to an ominous piece of art instead of just landscape.

"So how long do you think it would take the others to find us here?" Winnie asked carefully, as she shifted her staff from its resting place on her shoulder.

"Probably ten, maybe twenty minutes," Disana answered as she overturned another rock in search of the elusive plant.

"Good," Winnie said, pulling the cord on the flare. As the glowing white streak shot high into the heavens and exploded, illuminating the area, she added, "That's more than enough time for you to give me the antidote and leave, either by your choice or not."

"What? Winnie, I know I made a few comments, but…"

"Disana, don't play with me. The idea that there's an Imperial squad waiting with a dart specifically designed to kill a Gold-mooner, should one happen to pass by on a ship, is a stretch. And since you were carrying it, you'd have a cure just in case you accidentally were poisoned yourself. So give it here, and I won't have to take it. Personally I hope I have to take it, which is why I followed you out where no one would hold me back."

Disana smiled and spoke slowly. "I am impressed, Winnie. I had hopes that by acting attracted to the Triblood, you would second-guess any suspicions you had of me after I found him poisoned as you *wanting* me to be the one who did it. What gave it away?"

"Lunen has been one of the nicest people to both of us," Winnie said, a small smile on her lips, "but I still know him better than you, and he knows how to hold a grudge. One time I dumped a bucket of water on his head; he used his Blue-mooning to hit me with five buckets' worth."

"That still explains nothing."

"He wasn't reaching at you because he liked you. He was clawing at the air because he wanted to hurt you. Lunen's the only guy I know who would still try to strike someone who hurt him, regardless of the pain. Sadly, I'm going to have to act in his place."

"Not curious as to whom I really am?" Disana asked, reaching a hand into her robe.

"Does it matter?" Winnie asked.

"I wasn't lying when I said I loved you, Winnie," Disana said, producing a small vial attached to what looked like a leather choker. "Honestly, after this assignment was over, I would have been happy making you my pet." She tied the choker around her neck. "My brother is merciful, for he was the one who raised me after our parents died. He took me as his right hand, taught me the art of assassination. I'm one of the few who knows his true face, his true name.

"Your brother is…" Winnie started to ask, only to have Disana answer for her.

"My master and lover, the Masked Emperor," she stated, a proud gleam in her eye.

"Your lover?" Winnie couldn't believe what she heard. "You're both more twisted than I could have imagined. Still, doesn't explain why you targeted us."

"He learned of the Triblood's involvement in the battle against Imakur in the South. He also learned of a girl who seemed to be more than she appeared. My assignment was to learn what I could about you, and, if necessary, kill the Triblood at least. I trailed the ship and learned its destination, then all that was left was to get myself in some kind of trouble so that the gallant heroes would aid me."

"So you led me out here to kill me."

"No. I was hoping that they'd leave us alone, and I could offer you a place with me at the Emperor's side. My brother is generous, letting me have my own playthings for when he's not around. If you refused, I would have killed you afterward. Seems I'll have no choice now." She practically sang the last sentence, her smile reaching the corners of her mouth as her eyes shed the sad look they had when Winnie first met her. Sadism and madness were all that remained.

She only has Gold-moons. She's no stronger or faster than you are.

"The vial, Disana," Winnie growled as she brought her staff to a defensive position.

"You'll have to take it yourself," Disana responded, quickly drawing a throwing dagger from her robes and launching it at Winnie.

Subconsciously, Winnie had recognized the motion of a throw. That was the only explanation she had for why things seemed to blur and she had moved out of the way, allowing the blade to soar past her shoulder without a scratch. She felt herself exhale in sheer fright that she'd been *that* close to actually being stabbed.

Don't think. As soon as you dodge, attack in turn.

Winnie charged as Lunen's words rang in her head, rushing forward with her staff held behind her. Disana brought her hands over her head with a venomous smile and produced a pair of steel batons. As she brought them down with the intention of smashing Winnie's skull, her target quickly shifted on her feet and leapt to the right, swinging her staff in a wide arc. The thura-bone staff not only managed to deflect the batons but also threw Disana off balance. As she stumbled, Winnie instinctively pivoted on the balls of her feet, following up on the momentum from her swing. She gripped her staff with both hands and swung over her head, adding to the momentum of the weapon. It landed with a sickening *crack* on the assassin's left shoulder blade, and she quickly pointed the tip of the staff at Disana's head.

"Give me the antidote, and we can avoid this," Winnie gently pleaded.

"That disgusting Triblood didn't teach you the futility of fighting a Gold-mooner, did he?" Disana spat, a crackling sound emanating from her injured shoulder before she lashed out, knocking the staff out of her way. She then stepped forward, slamming her right baton into Winnie's side. Winnie was thankful her ribs didn't crack, but the pain was more than she was used to.

If your opponent gets close enough to strike you, that just means he's close enough for you to strike back.

Winnie quickly retaliated with her left fist, and even as her wrist hurt from the still-unperfected punch, she felt the satisfying crunch of a nose breaking. But Disana quickly retreated, shifting one baton to the other hand so she could pull her nose back in place. In an instant, there was no sign it had ever been broken.

"You can't do enough damage to matter, Winnie," she mocked. "You're not strong enough to really make it count, and you don't have the will to outlast me."

What your opponent thinks of you doesn't matter, whether they look down at or up to you. All that matters is the fight you give each other.

"At least I'm not built like a twelve-year-old girl," Winnie responded, bringing her staff back to a ready position. Disana shrieked as she lunged at Winnie. As the staff blocked repeated blows from both batons, Winnie realized she might have actually hit on a sore issue for the assassin.

There are always conditions for victory or failure, even if it's simply lasting until the fight is over. Keep in mind what it means to lose, and make sure that it doesn't happen.

As Winnie quickly ducked, she swung her leg out, hoping to trip Disana and finally have a chance to retrieve the antidote. But the Gold-mooner leapt over the sweep, bringing her batons down in yet another attempt to smash Winnie's head. Winnie quickly brought her staff up to block but didn't expect the knee that followed. She rolled with the attack but still felt the impact against her forehead. Her vision began to blur as her glasses flew from her face, but she felt sure her vision would've been blurred regardless. As she landed on her back, she felt the staff slip from her grip and could vaguely hear Disana speaking as she strode toward her.

"I'm sorry, Winnie, but there's only so much one with no moon can do, and there's no way a girl with no experience can fight a seasoned killer and honestly hope to win." She then gave Winnie a kick in the stomach, giggling at the cry of pain from her fallen opponent. "I could kill you, but then where would the pain be? Better I leave you here for them to find, alone with the knowledge that you failed." With that, she began to walk away.

I'm sorry Lunen. I wasn't good enough.

"How are you not good enough?"

"I'm not," Winnie answered on her hands and knees, her first training session with Lunen temporarily on hold. "I never stuck with anything that I just couldn't do."

"How do you know you're not good at something if you don't keep trying?" he asked, squatting down to look her in the eye. "The only difference between a true champion and just some random fool is the will to get back up when they're beaten down. All you need is encouragement."

"Life is never that perfect," she responded bitterly.

"Who was your greatest supporter as a child?" he asked.

"My mother, before she died," Winnie said, really unsure where this conversation was going.

"My parents always encouraged me before they died," he said. "So, when I was in the arena, and even after then, I always like to think they're watching me. That way, I can't just stay down during a fight. After all, they're rooting for me."

As Disana walked away, a small rock flew into the base of her skull. As she tumbled, she began to turn, her weapons falling from her hands. What she saw was not what she expected.

Well, I hope you enjoy the show, Mom. "I don't think we're done yet," Winnie said as she pushed her glasses back up the bridge of her nose, blood still trickling from her forehead. "Come on, Disana. Are you going to take that from someone with no moon?"

Disana charged, and Winnie quickly brought her foot up in a crescent kick that cracked across the deranged girl's face. As the assassin fell, Winnie quickly tackled her. As they wrestled, Winnie repeatedly punched her foe in the face, hoping to at least knock her out. Disana quickly shifted her body, throwing Winnie off, and began scrambling for her batons. Winnie quickly leapt onto her back and yanked at her long black hair. She then quickly reached down and squeezed the assassin's windpipe, only for Disana to once again shift position and throw her off.

"You can't defeat me," Disana said, standing up. "You're not good enough to win this fight."

"Already did," Winnie said with a smile, holding the antidote vial between her fingers. As Disana stared, dumbfounded, Winnie gave a shrill whistle.

"What was that supposed to do?" Disana asked as she drew a dagger from her robe.

"How many weapons do you actually carry?" Winnie asked incredulously.

Suddenly the familiar roar of a sky-lynx filled the air, and both girls turned to see Wind-hunter soaring in the distant heavens, Liana, Leito, and Zeg following on foot.

"She's the one who poisoned Lunen!" Winnie screamed before smiling at Disana.

"There will be a reckoning for this, my pet," Disana growled before sprinting to the cliff. As she dived, her robes unfolded, forming a makeshift parachute.

"Oh, you have got to be kidding," Winnie said as she gazed over the edge of the cliff. "How can she possibly…bring that much… just to kill two people…?"

And with that, fatigue finally caught up with the girl. As the others quickly made their way to her position, Winnie barely had time to hold the vial up and say "Antidote…" before passing out.

"So, you and Lunen brought an assassin onto *my* ship, who managed to not only poison Lunen but actually make her way all over the *Freewind*?" Liana asked through gritted teeth.

"Pretty much," Winnie answered as Migs finished binding her head. Her wrist was not sprained, and she'd managed to avoid any long-term damage to her torso. As she sat in the doctor's examination room, with Lunen slowly recovering on the bed in the corner, she almost wished she were unconscious so that she could avoid explaining things to the captain.

"Captain, I think we should be more concerned with why the Empire is taking more of an interest in this ship," Leito added.

"Let's be honest," Liana responded, "having the Empire want us dead just means the resistance will pay more for our services. But the fact that she got on the ship just means that Lunen isn't allowed to recruit anymore."

"It was my fault too," Winnie said as Migs finally left her to check on Lunen. "Honestly, I didn't think the sadness in her eyes was a lie. I think that if her twisted brother didn't turn her into his bedroom hit woman, she could have been a good person."

"I swear, if you suggest that she be allowed to join the crew…" Liana began.

"Captain, I swear, if I see her again, I'm going to finish the beating I owe her."

A week had passed since Winnie's fight with Disana, and Lunen was still sleeping on the deck when he felt something poking his ribs. As his eyelids fluttered, he saw the still-bandaged Winnie standing over him, using her staff as a cane.

"It's a little early, y'know…" Lunen yawned.

"We were marked for death by the Emperor," Winnie responded. "I don't know about you, but I need a lot more work if I'm going to have to face Disana again."

As Lunen stood up and stretched, he asked her, "So you're training because you're scared?"

"Not really," she answered. "I have people to protect, and people watching me. I need to get stronger if I'm not going to let them all down."

Lunen just smiled; she smiled back. She would never admit it aloud, but she was beginning to think that she did have a talent for at least protecting others, and that was something she knew her mother would be proud of.

*****

Far away, in a castle floating in the sky, Disana knelt before a man on a throne. Dressed completely in black as his long, unkempt black hair hung from his head, he glared at her from behind a black mask that hid all his features. As she stared into the red lenses that hid his eyes, she felt that her life was no longer in her hands.

"So, you failed to kill a newmooner and a Triblood?" he growled, his voice like gravel falling downhill.

"The Triblood was easy enough to poison, but I underestimated the girl," she quietly responded, averting her eyes from his gaze. "I thought she was as weak in spirit as she was in her moons."

He lifted his hand, and she felt her body lift into the air. As he stretched his fingers, her limbs began to pull out of their sockets. Tears rolled from her eyes as her limbs began to twist around. Had the pain not been overwhelming, she would have screamed.

"My lord," an attendant spoke, "I'm afraid that we are out of thura meat."

The red lenses turned from Disana, and she fell. He closed his fist, and the attendant's torso burst in a torrent of blood.

"You should thank my attendant, little sister," he said, rising from his throne. "While I had hoped you would not succeed in your assignment, I was still stunned at how overwhelmingly you failed."

"What do you mean, my beloved brother?" she whimpered, not bothering to lift herself up from the heap she'd landed in.

"I have plans for the Triblood and the girl," he said, raising a finger and drawing Disana to her feet. "If they did die, they would be useless for my plans—and you managed to discover that one can be used to force the other into doing what I need of them."

"So I did not fail you, my lord?" she asked cautiously.

He pulled the mask from his face, and drew closer to her lips. "You can't fail when you weren't supposed to succeed, dear sister."

Even after the battle in the Southern wastes, I didn't believe I was even capable of fighting, for others or myself. I owed Disana because if she hadn't poisoned Lunen, I wouldn't have discovered my talent there. And, of course, I owed her for giving me something to make fun of Lunen about for a long time. No guy could live down that his first kiss also tried to kill him.

CHAPTER 7: Blood and Steel

Winnie tried to not speak too much of things that existed only on her world. Sometimes explaining something, like an automobile or cinema, made her feel very idiotic. She was convinced that if her friends on the crew did not know she was from another world, they would have believed she was. As such, she kept discussing her world to a minimum. However, she discovered that stories, no matter where they were from, somehow drew and attracted people.

As such, she found herself explaining what she remembered of Shakespeare to Lunen one night in a village tavern near the border of the Vast Desert of the Red continent. She was enjoying a glass of what looked like tomato juice, but tasted closer to orange juice, while Lunen drank a glass of water. When she asked why he never seemed to drink anything but water at a tavern, he stated that a man who can set things on fire should never be drunk. When she asked if he'd ever set himself on fire while drunk, he quickly asked her about tales of warriors from her world.

“So let me see if I get this right,” Lunen said after taking a sip of water. “This Titus guy, instead of beating these men to death for what they did to his daughter, cooks them and feeds them to their mother?”

“Yeah.”

“That’s just...crazy,” he muttered.

“There was a question about his sanity at this point?” Winnie asked.

“There’s getting retribution, and then there’s just taking it too damn far.”

“Oh, so you don’t believe that there are some people so evil they should be punished?”

“I never said that, but to take lives needlessly is pointless and cruel, and something that should only be done as a last resort.”

“Oh, come on. What about what happened to your parents?” she asked as she stood up.

“What happened to them was monstrous and evil,” he shouted, standing up as well, “but I should never have lost control like that!”

“So you’re saying you wouldn’t have killed him for what he did to them if you didn’t lose control?” Winnie asked. “You never thought that if you let him live, he would’ve just kept hurting people?”

“I don’t have to wonder about it,” Lunen said evenly. “He’s dead. You saying I should just give out death and judgment all the time as I see fit?”

“We have a saying where I’m from: evil men succeed when good men do nothing!” she shouted, tossing her drink in his face. She then stormed out of the tavern.

Liana strolled over to Lunen and offered him a rag from the barman. As he dried off, she simply said, “While I know you two switch between being best friends and bickering twits as often as the sun sets, I've never seen her just walk off like that."

"She talked down to me, just because I make sure to avoid killing anyone if I can help it," he muttered.

"Considering how often you've risked your life for her, do you really think it was looking down at you, or fear for your safety?"

"What do you..."

"Lunen, she does share a room with me now, and we do talk at night. She does worry about you. She's worried that one day, you're going to hold back and it's going to get you killed."

A moment of silence passed before Lunen dropped the rag and left to chase after Winnie.

Liana just smiled. "To watch him beg for an apology, or not? Maybe I'll get some of the crew together so we can all have a laugh."

As Winnie made her way through the town's market, she kept twirling her staff, trying to work out the frustration from her conversation with Lunen. She never admitted a lot of her feelings about the Triblood, but the one she was adamant about was that he was something of a hero. In the time since she'd met him, he had saved her life several times, as well as the lives of various people on the crew. The battle in the South, his return at the Zero Point, all of it had arranged in her mind to tell her that he was like something from cartoons she watched as a child.

But this is the real world—one of them, anyway—and how long before he ends up getting killed trying to be the good guy?

She continued winding her way through the marketplace with no real destination. She just kept trying to decide whether Lunen was too nice, or too stupid.

I mean, it makes sense if I killed people in self-defense. After all, this world is dangerous and no one could blame me. But how can he keep such ideas of morality when he's lost so much?

She sighed as she came to a stop, wondering if Lunen just handled loss better than she imagined she would if she went through the same experiences he had.

"Where is Lunen?"

The question woke her from her thoughts, and she turned to see what looked like a large man threatening one of the merchants. He stood about six and a half feet tall and wore a long, black, hooded cape. The hood hid his face, but his arms were the color of bronze, and very muscular. On his back, he wore a sword in a strange scabbard, one that had an opening along its length for easy removal. A foot-long chain hung from its pommel, and its hilt-guard was long in both directions and perfectly perpendicular to the blade. The blade itself was of average width, but it was almost as long as the hooded man was tall. With the sword's grip being long enough for three hands to hold it, Winnie would have thought he was compensating for something. The edge in his voice as he spoke again made her realize that she should probably stop thinking of jokes and run.

"I've seen that the ship called *Freewind* is here. Where is its Triblood? Where is Lunen?"

Winnie quickly turned and ran back to the tavern. She rounded a shop and put more speed into her step but paused as she heard a sound. With the realization that it was the sound of a fluttering cape *above* her, she leapt back as the hooded man landed with both feet passing through where her head had been only a moment earlier.

"Tell me, girl with a staff of bone," he said, pulling his hood back to reveal a bronze skin, golden eyes, and long, spiked white hair, "are you the infamous companion of Lunen? You match the rumors I've heard. Where is he?"

Winnie quickly brought her staff to a defensive position. "If I were, why would I tell you?"

"Because," he said, his right hand reaching up to the hilt of his sword, "if you don't tell me, I'll have to break each bone in your body until your screams draw him."

He took a step toward her but paused. Then he smiled and again leapt into the air. A streak of fire collided with the spot he'd been standing on. As he landed on the roof of a small shop, his smile widened. Winnie followed both his gaze and the path the flame had taken to see Lunen standing on a roof across the road from the one the strange man stood on.

"The infamous undefeated champion of Lohl's arena," he exhaled, a hint of manic joy in his voice. "The son of the great Redmoon warrior who learned every bare-handed fighting style in the world, Kabern. The Triblood Lunen."

"White hair, black cape, and a ridiculously overcompensating sword," Lunen commented. "So that would make you the Fight-Hunter Izoln, wouldn't it?"

"You've heard of me. I'm so glad," Izoln said, his insane smile threatening to split his face.

"A lunatic who hunts great warriors for the thrill is the kind of story an old arena-fighter like me wouldn't just ignore." Lunen replied as he cracked his knuckles before turning his attention to Winnie. "Tell Liana to get the ship started. This shouldn't take long."

"If anything, you've got guts, Triblood," Izoln said, stretching his neck around with a few satisfying pops from the bones. "Let's see how your skills match up."

"Let's," Lunen retorted, thrusting his open palm at his opponent, a blast of wind emanating from it. Izoln quickly leapt over the blast, soaring at the Triblood. Lunen threw a punch, but Izoln quickly intercepted his attack with a punch of his own, throwing Lunen backwards and sending him bouncing back and forth between the narrow walls of an alley. As he tried to shake off the grogginess from the blow, he saw Izoln land in front of him, his arms hidden beneath his cloak.

"Was that honestly the best opening attack you could do, or were you holding back because of the girl?" Izoln asked, his voice reflecting a genuine desire to know.

"Does it matter?" Lunen asked, coughing.

Izoln shrugged. "I heard that despite your…limitations, in both moons and training, you were something interesting."

Izoln quickly braced himself as Lunen managed to launch himself from what appeared to be a prone position on the floor. Apparently the Triblood wanted to pay him back with a punch of his own. As Lunen's right fist advanced, Izoln's right hand quickly gripped him by the wrist. Securing an additional grip under the Triblood's bicep, he redirected the momentum and launched Lunen over his head and straight through the wall of a house. A bolt of lightning shot from the damaged structure, and Izoln leapt to the side. He smiled, impressed at his own ability to dodge what traditionally was impossible to escape.

His smile faded as Lunen tackled him in midair, sending them both smashing through another house. Izoln slammed his elbow into Lunen's back, while the Triblood responded by tightening his grip and igniting them both in flames. Both combatants disengaged, with Izoln slamming into one of the only surviving walls with enough force to suffocate the fire. Lunen threw his arms out and wind swirled around him, putting his own burning body out.

"My God! It's so damned strange!" Izoln's voice was filled with the joy of discovering a new understanding of something. "You're both overrated and underrated at the same damn time!"

"What the hell are you going on about?" Lunen asked, struggling to maintain his footing.

"Your reputation is based solely on you being more than what your opponents expected," the Fight-Hunter said, rotating his shoulders as if this were merely an exercise. "You have little refined skill in fighting techniques, but you make up for it with creative uses of your moons and raw instinct. Your strength combined with your ability to survive, and to use the elements as well…It's enough to make me overlook your obvious limits."

"I'm sorry," Lunen responded through gritted teeth. "Limits?"

"Single Blue-mooners can't form the elements into complex shapes, and no way can they use earth unless it's small and loose, like sand. And you have no real training, so a skilled fighter who isn't underestimating you can obviously beat you."

Lunen launched himself at Izoln in a rage. What no one knew about Lunen was that he had not learned to fight in the arena. His father had taught his basic skill set to him as a child. And, like almost all boys, Lunen saw his father as someone to both idealize and eventually surpass. As long as he lived, he would not allow anyone to insult the memory of his father telling him how to punch, grapple, and block.

Izoln grinned and lashed out with a vicious roundhouse kick, sending the Triblood through yet another wall and skidding down the street, the Fight-Hunter following behind him. As Lunen tried to pick himself up, Izoln pulled his right leg back and began to rotate his ankle inward. Lunen screamed in pain as he felt a few ligaments tear and quickly propped himself up on his hands and struck Izoln's face with his left heel.

As Izoln backpedaled, clutching his face, the Triblood attempted to stand. His ankle hurt but could still support some of his weight. He then launched several wind-cuts at his opponent. Izoln quickly reached over his shoulder and drew his massive sword, swinging it with such force that he shattered the wind-cuts. Lunen stared in disbelief. He knew in his heart that no ordinary sword should have been able to deflect that attack.

"What is that thing?" Lunen asked, already afraid that he knew the answer.

"You like it?" Izoln responded.

"Didn't your mother teach you not to answer a question with another one?" Lunen replied wryly but regretted the question when he saw Izoln's demeanor change. As Izoln charged the Triblood with his massive sword, Lunen quickly drew his dagger. The two weapons rang as they collided, and Lunen was thrown back as Izoln skidded to a stop.

Then Lunen heard a soft *crack*, and it took him a moment to realize it had come from the weapon in his hand. He gazed at his father's weapon, refusing to believe it could be damaged, and realized the truth of Izoln's sword.

"That's a Blood-Steel sword, isn't it?" Lunen asked.

"The same as your father's dagger," Izoln replied. "Forged with the blood of its owner in the metal by the Blood-Forgers of Crescent Canyon, the weapons take on different forms and abilities based on the person they belong to. Only a Blood-Steel weapon's master can bring out its true potential, and, in their hands, it's *unbreakable.*"

Izoln smirked, and began to wrap the chain dangling from his sword's pommel around his forearm. As he tightened it, the veins on his arm began to swell and the sword's blade began to vibrate slightly. As he gripped it with both hands, the smirk widened again into that insane smile.

"This is my weapon, Piercing Resonance," he said dangerously. He then leapt into the air. "And this is its power!"

Lunen dived forward, narrowly avoiding the blade as it stabbed into the spot where he'd just stood. He'd expected a sword of that length to be used like a spear. He had not expected the ground beneath him to rupture and collapse, creating a wide crater.

"A Blood-Steel weapon in the hands of anyone else is just a toy," Izoln said mockingly, the chain dangling again from the pommel as he stood in the center of the crater.

Lunen threw his dagger at Izoln, hoping it would pierce his heart before the Fight-Hunter could wrap the chain around his forearm again. Izoln quickly swung his sword, smashing the dagger in two.

Lunen's chest began to hurt, and he felt his eyes tearing up. That dagger was all he truly had left from his father. He did not even realize he had shot the lightning that struck Izoln's arm, forcing him to drop the sword, and as his body leapt at his enemy and his right fist pulled back to give the hardest punch he had ever given, it felt as if he was watching someone else control his actions. He only became aware again that this was no dream as Izoln threw his own right fist at Lunen's. As their fists collided, both combatants screamed in agony as the bones from their knuckles to their shoulders fractured.

Lunen fell to his knees while Izoln stumbled a little before regaining his footing. The Triblood watched apathetically as his opponent walked slowly to pick up his sword with his left hand. Lunen did not care anymore. He was more than just beaten; he was outclassed in every single way. It was one thing to lose. It was another to fail so epically, unable to even warrant a decent second attempt. For the first time in his life, Lunen simply did not care about trying anymore.

Before Izoln could pick up his weapon, he heard a scream. He turned in time to see Winnie slam her staff into the side of his head. As he stumbled backward, Liana leapt over Winnie, bringing both feet with crushing force into the Fight-Hunter's ribs. Izoln landed on his back. If he remained conscious, he was doing a superb job of not showing it.

Lunen felt his cheeks burn as both girls forced him to his feet. He did not want to be seen like this, so pathetic and broken. He barely managed to mutter, "My father's dagger," to Winnie, who quickly grabbed the pieces before they dragged him back to the ship.

Izoln blinked a few times as sunlight began to warm his face and winced as he tried to move his right arm. He fumbled with his left hand, in the folds of his charred and frayed cloak, for a leather bag with a metal cylinder at its tip. As he drank the bitter red liquid, he kept reminding himself that it would accelerate his healing. That thought, along with the plan to chase Lunen down and finish the fight, was what kept him from spitting it out.

"Stupid Triblood," he muttered as he picked up his sword, sheathing it over his shoulder. "Stupid people saving him...I would've won if they'd just stayed out of it."

He thought about the fractured mess that was his right arm. Izoln could not deny that, for all the disadvantages the Triblood had from the beginning, he'd managed to score an impressive blow, even though it had injured him as well. That was reason enough for the Fight-Hunter to track him down and finish it. He was smart enough to know where Lunen would logically go, and that it would take about a week on foot to head somewhere it would take a few days to reach by airship.

"How is he, Migs?" Winnie asked. Lunen had not spoken since asking her to retrieve his dagger. Given Lunen's tendency to talk whether you wanted him to or not, that was worrisome. And this time, there was no aquatic horror to explain why he was being this way. So when the doctor returned to the deck to speak with Liana, Winnie, and Leito, she was eager to know what was happening.

"The ligaments in his ankle were slightly torn, and he has hairline fractures and soft tissue damage in several areas. His arm is quite literally in pieces," Migs answered, removing his gloves and pushing his glasses up. He turned his head to take in the view of the skies. "However, that is not the most distressing aspect of this recent altercation."

"He hasn't spoken to you either," Winnie confirmed. She was starting to feel nervous and unconsciously began running her thumbs along the rest of her fingers.

"He's just being a brat," Liana said with a superficial smile. She wrapped her arms around her torso as the cool winds began to blow. "I'm sure that in a few days, he'll be bugging us all over again."

"Begging your pardon, Captain," Winnie said, "but that's bullshit and you know it."

"First off, what the hell is a bull?" Liana said, turning to face Winnie. "And second, I think he's pulled this crap once before, remember?"

"This is different from the Zero Point, Liana," Winnie replied. "At least then he was showing emotion. He's too damn quiet for it to be all right."

"He wasn't just beaten," Leito said at last. He sighed, as if ready to give an uncomfortable explanation. "He was utterly overwhelmed in skill. I don't think he's ever faced someone who outclassed him and wasn't stupid enough to underestimate him. And, if what Winnie says is true, the comparisons to his father wouldn't help the situation at all."

"Just who was that guy anyway?" Winnie asked.

"Izoln the Fight-Hunter," Liana began. She began to pace back and forth from rail to rail as she spoke. "They say that his mother was a Gold-mooner who came to the Red continent to seek her fortune. And apparently, some crazed bandit leader who thought he was a warlord raped her. After that, Izoln was born, under a Red half-moon, with his father's full Red-moon and mother's Gold half-moon in his blood. Rather than abandon him, his mother raised and loved him. But the village she settled in knew who his father was. They blamed the child for everything and eventually drove them out into the desert. All we can know is that his mother died, and he returned to the village and burned it to the ground."

"My God," Winnie gasped, her hand covering her mouth in shock.

"Well, that's how the story goes," Liana added. "And don't interrupt. So apparently he starts traveling around the world, finding and learning combat arts from anyone he can. They even say he got a Blood-Steel weapon…"

"Given the damage we could see from the airship, Captain, he probably does have one," Leito added as his eyes glanced toward the area where Migs came from. Winnie saw concern in his eyes, as if he shared her thoughts on facing someone so dangerous alone.

"Am I ever going to finish this story?" Liana asked. "Anyway, so he gets all these skills and gets the weapon, and finally he tracks down his father and kills him. After that, the story gets a little weird. He starts going after anyone who has a reputation for fighting and kills them all in combat. No sneak attacks, no tricks. Just his skills and weapons against everything they have."

"So, he'll leave Lunen alone?" Winnie asked.

"Not likely," Leito replied. "You said his arm looked as injured as Lunen's. That's something he's going to want to avenge."

"If he's going to come after Lunen again," Winnie said, turning to head to Migs's examination room, "we need to get him back on his feet."

"You have to give her credit," Migs said as they watched her walk off. "She is as stubborn as he is."

My God…It was a sight Winnie had never expected to see. Lunen's entire upper torso was bandaged as he sat on the bed, as was his elevated right foot. His arm was not only bandaged but held in several splints. A wire hung from the ceiling, keeping the shattered limb elevated. What truly worried her was that Lunen's eyes, always fiery and intense, had become dull and uncaring.

"So…" she started, already regretting the words as they left her mouth, "how're you feeling?" When he did not react, she took a chair and sat next to him. "I know you're in pain now, but you'll be ready next time."

"There won't be a next time," Lunen muttered.

"Come on," she replied, trying her best to sound reassuring. "You're the guy who never gives up."

"I know," he said quietly. "But I never..." He brought his left hand up to his face, and Winnie turned away briefly. She could understand him not wanting to be seen crying.

"I mean, so what if you lost?" she asked. "I mean, that just means you have to try harder next time."

"Winnie..." he said. "I keep thinking that if my father didn't die saving me, he could have finished teaching me how to fight. Izoln's fighting style is a lot like his was. Mixing concepts from different schools of martial thought...hell, even using a Blood-Steel weapon is like my father."

"You mean his dagger?"

"He told me once its name was Swift Strike. With a single touch, it could cut anything. It was his last resort." He wiped his eyes again. "Honestly, he only killed opponents when there was no other way. I'm not as good as he was."

"No one expects you to be him," she said, touching his uninjured hand, finally understanding Lunen's choice to not kill if he could help it.

"I know," he replied. "But if there was a warrior worth trying to be, it was him."

"Maybe you can still get better," Winnie said. "Maybe you can be like your dad, but in your own way."

"Winnie, even if I trained like he did, it doesn't change the fact that I will still be lacking against Izoln if we fight again."

"Well, we could always get your dagger remade," she commented, not liking that Lunen's eyes had not regained their light and intensity. As much as she hated to admit, she preferred the willful warrior as opposed to this broken, hurt person. She hoped that at least restoring his father's keepsake would reignite his passion, if not just make him smile again.

"Like Liana will go out of her way to Crescent Canyon just to remake an heirloom," he muttered dejectedly.

"If she wants me to stop bugging her she will," Winnie replied with a small, reassuring smile.

After a few hours of ragged debate, Winnie finally managed to talk Liana into taking them to Crescent Canyon. After all, the opportunity to visit one of the most renowned people in the world, as pointed out by Leito, could be a once-in-a-lifetime opportunity. And, of course, Liana translated that as something she could advertise to potential clients. And if she could somehow open the Blood-Forgers up to the idea of shipping and trade, she would be rich. It was at moments like that that Winnie appreciated how Liana's financial lunacy helped out more than hindered the crew.

During the few days it took to reach Crescent Canyon, Winnie attempted to reignite Lunen's will, with no success. Leito reminded her that Lunen's depression had some justification. While Lunen could train to be good enough to fight Izoln one day, it would take years that he did not have if they were right about the Fight-Hunter coming after him.

"You couldn't get him ready in time?" she asked the first mate.

"I could teach him some things, but it would take a genius of combat to get Lunen ready in the short time we have—and those are of short supply."

Winnie contemplated this as the ship descended toward Crescent Canyon, a landscape as illogical as most things she saw on this world. As she always understood, rivers eating away at the earth for centuries formed canyons. However, Crescent Canyon seemed abnormal from the sky because it made a single perfect crescent moon shape. There was no additional cut in the ground, and Winnie learned it was because this canyon had no river.

According to the stories, the Blood-Forgers were originally the only order of mystics on the Red Continent. They focused their strength toward developing the spirit, and they had even begun to learn methods of using a person's blood to tell possible futures, for as they often said, fate was not made by the moons but by the heart. After years of persecution, they had settled in the area of the Vast Desert that would become Crescent Canyon. They say that the order tore at the ground with hammer and pick until they made a secure home too dangerous for any army to invade.

After carving the canyon, they built their city within the earth, an entire subterranean culture. After settling, the mystics found a suitable way to serve the people of the world—by using the blood of a person in the forging of steel. This gave the steel properties that were unique to the blood. In time, the order became more eccentric as they isolated themselves from the world, choosing to only make weapons of Blood-Steel for those they thought deserving of it. What those qualifications were was a mystery, and no one knew what their policies were on remaking what they had already forged.

As the *Freewind* landed close to the center of the outside curve, Liana gave the crew its orders. A group of twenty-five, including herself, Leito, Lunen, Winnie, and Migs, would descend to the Blood-Forgers' city. Meanwhile, the rest, led by Zeg, would keep an eye out for trouble, be it the Empire, or Izoln. Wind-hunter was left behind especially for the purpose of sniffing out the Fight-Hunter, since he had memorized the scent on Lunen after he saw his broken body.

"Um, Captain?" Winnie said as she helped Lunen down to the ground, sweating from both the effort and the desert's noon sun. "How are we supposed to get down there?"

"Offhand," Liana replied with a grin, pointing to what looked like a stairway carved into the rocky surface, "I'd say on these."

"Right. Remind me not to talk again, right Lunen?" Winnie said with a chuckle of embarrassment as she supported both her weight and Lunen's with the help of her staff. She stopped laughing when she realized that Lunen still was not reacting with any of his usual humor or encouragement.

As they descended, Leito gave an impressed whistle as he saw all the mirrors lining the wall they descended, all pointing at various angles. On the next wall, across a great distance, they saw even more mirrors, as well as several openings in the canyon's side leaking steam.

"Ingenious," Migs gasped, shocking Winnie since she'd *never* seen him gasp. "The mirrors reflect sunlight, if not all light, into the city. I am willing to wager that they have some kind of massive reflection device to distribute the light throughout the area."

"Well, at least we aren't dealing with some kind of hideous subterranean monsters, right?" Winnie said, hoping to provoke a laugh from Lunen. All she got was a tired look. "Y'know, I remember when you made all the insanity seem fun," she mumbled.

After a half-hour, they finally reached the bottom. Several robed figures stood waiting for them, standing before a twenty-foot-high and fifteen-foot-wide door. The only weapons they seemed to have were several large forging hammers, ironically. Winnie imagined they used them more like war hammers.

"Greeting, Blood-Forgers," Liana began, hoping her voice sounded both confident and respectful. "I am Captain Liana Revolzin of the free trading ship *Freewind*, and I hope that we can open a fair and honest trade."

"The captain has a last name?" Winnie asked in shock. After all the time she'd spent on the ship, she'd never heard anyone use a surname. It briefly made her wonder what Lunen's could be.

"Winnie, shut up," Liana said before continuing. "As I was saying, the way I see things, your people may be in need of supplies, and we're willing to help bring supplies when you need them. And all I ask in exchange is..."

A very short robed figure quickly approached Liana and offered her hand. Liana looked over her shoulder at the others before looking down again and reaching down to shake the small person's hand. Liana shrieked and jumped back, reaching for her swords as her palm dripped blood. The small person did not move, however, choosing instead to stare at the bloodstains Liana had left on her hand by the hidden needle in the palm of her glove. Liana removed her hands from her blades. Winnie suspected it was because she had remembered that these people seemed to involve blood in all aspects of their lives.

"Your offer is a veil," the small person said at last, revealing her to be an elderly woman, "so you can help someone you consider a brother to regain his spirit."

Liana's cheeks flushed, and Winnie saw Lunen's head rise slightly.

"Before you ask, we cannot read the fates of men," the old woman said before any could speak, "we can only guess, based on what kind of person the blood tells us you are."

"Can you help or not?" Liana said quickly, hoping to avoid any comments from Lunen.

Winnie, despite the fact that Lunen was not acting like himself, could imagine the jokes: *so, does this mean I get the ship if you can't be captain anymore?* Winnie gave a bittersweet smile at the thought and deeply hoped that Lunen would snap out of this depression soon.

"Depends on what it is he needs," the elderly woman said, walking toward Lunen. Lunen slowly offered her his good hand, but she shook her head, took a short blade from her robe, and gave his forearm a small cut. She looked at the blood as intently as before and smiled. "We often wondered if you were coming, Son of Kabern."

"You knew my father?" Lunen asked, his silence broken at last.

"I am Ellamar, High Priestess of the Blood-Forgers," she answered, pulling her hood back to reveal a tanned, wrinkled yet lean face, a mischievous twinkle in her blue eyes as she watched from beneath a mane of white hair. She then turned, as did the rest of the robed people, and as the massive door opened, she added, "I was the one who forged your father's dagger."

Winnie had never told anyone, but the most beautiful sight she ever saw in her life was the view from the *Freewind* as it ascended to the same level as the clouds. While she had ridden in an airplane before, it did not compare to the panoramic view of the world from above as the airship soared. She believed that nothing she would see after would move her emotionally as much as that view. And as they followed Ellamar into the Blood-Forgers' city, she learned how wrong she was.

The first thing anyone would notice about the city was the humidity. As the Blood-Forgers removed their robes, revealing clothing that seemed built for long periods of time in hot, humid environments, Winnie found herself thankful she was already wearing the same clothes she wore for combat and training. Liana was tugging at her collar, and Migs unbuttoned part of his shirt. Leito didn't seem to mind the heat, and Winnie felt Lunen moving the air along his skin to keep himself cool. Once they passed the tunnel leading in, they saw the city proper.

Migs had been right about a large reflection device. A massive series of small crystals lined the center point of the high ceiling, refracting the light from the canyon openings so that the noon sun illuminated the entire city. As the light shone, it allowed the *Freewind* crew to see that the houses and various buildings were carved from the stone that had filled the area before the Blood-Forgers arrived. And in the far back of the cavernous city, rising above the houses and buildings like a watchful god, stood the Temple, one of the largest forges Winnie would ever see in her lifetime. It seemed to glow from the heat within, and steam traveled upward, riding along the ceiling and out the openings that let the light in. And it was there, up the long, imposing stairs, that Ellamar led them.

*****

“So I’m sure the girl supporting the Triblood has questions,” Ellamar said as she sat on the ground before a long, low table. She reached for a goblet, drinking deep the water there.

“How did you know that?” Winnie asked as they joined her.

“Your eyes say it all,” Ellamar answered, smiling.

“So, what exactly makes Blood-Steel different from other things?” Winnie asked, not wanting to be distracted by the old woman, who’d already made it clear she had no problems drawing blood from strangers.

“It’s mostly in the blood itself,” Ellamar answered, putting the goblet down. “Not just anyone’s blood can be used. There has to be passion, drive, and will, hidden or otherwise.”

“So, what else makes a person worthy of a weapon like that?”

“Honestly, it varies from high priest or priestess to the next.” Ellamar stood and walked over toward Lunen. “It’s mostly a sense of curiosity about what the person is like, what they can do with it.”

“Tell me about my father,” Lunen said suddenly, stepping away from Winnie. It was the first time he’d spoken since they had entered the city. “Why did you make Swift Strike for him?”

“Honestly, because he had no initial desire for it. When your father fell into our midst, quite literally, by the way, it took him days to recover. The whole time, he was respectful, and yet expressed no desire for an all-powerful weapon. That made me curious about what a weapon from a man who already made a name for himself on his warrior’s training journey would be like, if he didn’t do it for power.”

“So, Swift Strike was what?” Lunen asked, staring at her tanned face.

"A last resort, for if his skills weren't enough," she said. "Your father believed that a strong warrior protected as much as he could. That even included the lives of his enemies, unless there was no other way. We all mourned when we heard of the passing of such a noble man. And since then, I often thought that his rumored Triblood child would one day come."

Lunen looked crestfallen. Winnie could imagine how he must now be comparing himself to his father even more.

"Can you fix my father's dagger?" he asked at last, taking the two pieces from his sheath.

"What in the world happened to it?" she asked, her voice seeming more irritated than shocked.

After Lunen told her of his fight with Izoln, she shook her head.

"Why am I not surprised?" she asked. "I told him that if he focused all his goals on the death of his father, he'd just become another stupid warrior chasing someone worth fighting."

"What are you talking about?" Winnie asked, worrying what the answer could be.

"Izoln is not a bad person," Ellamar replied. "He just focused so much on getting revenge on his father that once he achieved it, he became lost."

"He's probably coming after me," Lunen said. "I'd like to get my father's dagger fixed and get out before trouble occurs."

"You're not going to fight him?" Ellamar asked.

"I can't face him. I'm not good enough yet," he said quietly.

"Ah, 'yet.' My favorite word in that statement," Ellamar replied with a smile. "It means you haven't given up yet in spirit." She picked up the pieces of the dagger. "I can't remake Swift Strike, as it was meant only for your father, but I could melt its metal down and use it to forge a weapon for you. That way, you can be prepared to face him."

"That won't make me ready for him as far as skill goes," Lunen replied as he began to turn away.

Ellamar smiled and rubbed her hands together. Lunen barely saw a hint of a glowing aura before she leapt up and punched him with enough force to knock him out. As he landed hard on his back, his eyes stayed open, glowing a bright blue.

"What the hell did you do?" Liana yelled, reaching for her swords.

"Put him in a spirit trance," Ellamar answered after cackling over her attack. Then she took a needle and stabbed it into Lunen's bicep. As she drew it out, his blood coated it. "There, that ought to be enough to forge him something. Oh, the spirit trance should help him prepare in time, with the aid of those long passed. In three days, he'll either be more skilled, or he'll be very angry with me."

"Did you have to punch him?" Winnie asked as she tried to reposition his body so he would be comfortable.

"Not really, but it should light a fire under his ass while he trains in spirit," the old woman replied before running off to the main forge, cackling all the while.

"Winnie," Liana said, glaring at her, "I will *never* listen to your ideas again when it comes to helping members of the crew."

"How was I supposed to know the high priestess was crazy?" Winnie replied in a panicked voice as they both walked away, leaving Lunen on the ground by the table.

As Lunen reeled from the blow, his vision blurred, but his thoughts remained fixed on the single intention of beating an old woman into submission. He realized the hypocrisy of trying to be a nice person but seeing nothing wrong with beating up the elderly, but one thing he'd learned in the arena was that if you threw an attack, you better be ready for retaliation of some kind.

As he regained his footing, the Triblood realized that something was not right with the situation. First, the soreness in his ankle was not there as he stumbled. It was as if it had already healed, too fast even for his blood. He flexed his right arm with no hint of the extensive damage it had suffered and took in his surroundings.

He stood in the center of a massive dusty circle. At the edge of the circle lay a trench. At the edge of that, a high wall, and curving from the top of that, a large bowl filled with benches of wood. He'd spent too many years of his life fighting there to not recognize the arena of Lohl. Lunen quickly turned, taking in the sight of it. For the ten years he'd fought there, he had never seen it empty. The sight made him more uneasy than the sight of it filled with people calling for blood and death.

"How did I get here?" he asked aloud. Then he looked up at the unnatural sun above him as it showered the area in blue light. He focused his ears and heard nothing but his own heartbeat and breath. In fact, his breath was the only moving air he felt. Then he finally heard the sound of footsteps on wood.

"You never really left here," a deep, imposing voice called. Lunen pivoted on his right heel, placing all his weight on it as he turned toward the source.

The figure wore a white cloak with crimson lining. Bandages concealed his face, except for his eyes. He wore no shirt, revealing that he was not only as tall as Leito but just as muscled. Lunen was sure that each of the man's shoulders was as big as his own head.

His pants, reaching only to his knees, were made of simple black cloth, but they were loose, ideal for rapid movement. He wore leather sandals fit for a warrior, long laces curving upward around his calves. Every muscle on his body was large, not ridiculously but enough to be imposing. The way he carried himself, Lunen knew, was the stride of a warrior with years of experience.

"Last I checked, I was done with this place when Lohl told me of his betrayal," Lunen retorted, taking a few steps back. If Izoln had beaten him as badly as he had, Lunen knew this man could destroy him on a whim.

"And yet your heart lingered here," the man said, his pace quickening. As he reached the high wall, he leapt clear over it and landed on the arena floor with enough force to kick up dust. "In every fight you had since you left, you still carried the fear this place put in you. You carried the fear of failing the ones you care for."

The man then charged forward with such speed that Lunen suspected him to be a full Red-mooner. The Triblood thrust his open hands forward, shooting a burst of flame, only to see his opponent quickly change direction and move around the attack. Lunen felt the blow before he saw it as an elbow crashed into the side of his head, and then he watched the strange blue world spin as he skidded and rolled along the floor at incredible speed. As he rolled to a stop, he saw the figure walking slowly toward him. He quickly leapt up, thrusting his fist at his opponent, and a cloud of dust rose as the wind attack connected. Lunen then opened his hands wide, shaping his fingers into claws and sending wave after wave of wind-cuts into the dust before preparing to shoot a bolt of lightning at whichever side the man chose to dive out from.

"Every fight, you keep thinking that if you lose, someone will die!"

The man burst from the dust cloud, heading straight at Lunen, blood dripping from his wounds as his now-torn cloak fluttered behind him. Lunen fired the lightning bolt straight at his heart—and watched in awe and horror as he *dived* over it. When the warrior hit the ground, he rolled and lashed out with two kicks as he balanced upright on his hands. One foot smashed into the side of Lunen's head; the second crashed into his shoulder blade as he spun with the blow, throwing him to the ground. The cloaked man somersaulted, extending his right foot with the intent of bringing it down on Lunen's throat. The Triblood quickly brought his hands up and ignited the air, burning the man's leg. His opponent twisted in midair, landing on his hands and quickly kicking out with his left leg, sending Lunen once more skidding along the ground.

"You won't be able to always save everyone, but if you fail, that just means you keep fighting and get stronger! You don't just cave in, you get better, find another way, scream your defiance to the heavens themselves and never give up, even in the face of failure!"

The man placed his burned foot on top of Lunen's chest and stared down at him.

"You only lost to Izoln because you thought yourself a failure to your father. The only advantage he had over you was training and a weapon. You have creativity, raw talent, and an unbreakable will. Your will only bent because you felt outclassed. The Blood-Forgers will take care of the weapon, while I'll train your talent and creativity in true skill. But you're the one who cannot turn away or back down."

"How do you know all that?" Lunen coughed. "What makes you think you know anything about me?"

"Because from the day you first opened your eyes until the day I finally closed mine, I knew that you had what it took to become even better than I was," the man said, reaching up and pulling the bandages from his face. Small, faint scars lined his flesh, and short black hair crowned his head. Beneath a round nose, a mustache grew and branched, forming a beard that hid his jaw from view. Lunen gazed up at the brown, burning eyes that he never could forget.

"Father?"

Ellamar stood over the molten steel as it heated and tossed the pieces of the dagger in. She then dropped the needle with Lunen's blood in as well and, with her gloved hands, picked up a large metal pole and began mixing the molten solution.

"Aren't you worried that the pole will melt?" Winnie asked as she wiped sweat from her brow.

"Did you choose not return to your ship because of curiosity, or concern?" Ellamar countered.

"A little of both," Winnie said, walking closer to the old woman. "So, why aren't you worried about the pole?"

"Because every tool a Blood-Forger uses is made with their own blood in it. And you've probably seen that a Blood-Steel object won't break in the hands of its master."

"Probably should have guessed," Winnie said. "Although I'm worried about Lunen having *anything* that won't break when he's using it."

"It's very strange," Ellamar commented. "I mean, despite the legacy he has from his parents, I never imagined that he'd have such friends."

"Because he's a Triblood?" Winnie asked, a little irritation in her voice.

"That as well, but mostly because, if he's that melancholic, I don't imagine people putting up with him."

"I see," Winnie said. "Well, honestly, even when he's down, he's a lot more positive than he's been lately. I think losing hurt his confidence more than he would want to admit."

"Failure is a harsh thing to experience," Ellamar said as she paused to stare at the molten metal as if trying to read what it wanted from her, "but sometimes, we learn to stand only by falling."

"Never really saw it that way," Winnie said as she dropped to one knee, hoping to see something in the metal that would give her a greater understanding of these people. "When I completely failed at something, it meant that I wasn't ever going to be good at it."

"Did you ever fail at something you love to do?" Ellamar asked, giving the girl a slight nudge as she began to change her position, stirring the metal more.

"I don't understand…"

"Was what you were failing at something you truly wanted, or was it something you just did? When I was your age, I couldn't read the blood, and I couldn't sing. I can read the blood but still can't sing. Guess which one was what I always wanted to do?"

"You wanted to read blood?" Winnie asked incredulously.

"I wanted to be high priestess, and I didn't give up on it, regardless of when I failed. I just got that much better for all my failures. And that's the only way to live if you want something hard enough. I'm sure you'll find what you truly want, and achieve it. And Lunen will regain whatever it is he lost, if he doesn't give up."

"I don't understand," Lunen said as his father helped him to his feet. "Am I dead?"

"No. From what I saw, that old lunatic was preparing another 'spirit trance punch,' and I figured I should hurry down as soon as you took the hit. Ellamar always seemed to get some perverse joy from punching people." Kabern answered, smiling as he looked at his son. "My God, it's wonderful to actually feel your hand, to see you as someone in front of me and not as if I was just an observer."

"You've been watching me this whole time?"

"The dead who have loved ones left continue to watch. You have no secrets from us."

"Is Mother here as well?" Lunen turned his head around rapidly, hoping to catch a glimpse of his other parent.

"I'm afraid that this trance is for a purpose, son," Kabern stated as he walked to his son, placing a hand on his shoulder. "Izoln is a few days from here, and he *will* try to finish the fight. And while Ellamar makes you a weapon, I'm going to make sure that the only thing that truly decides this fight will be willpower."

"Father, I can't become a master of combat in a few days."

"Lunen, your moons give you perfect balance of offense and defense, and your time in the arena helped you refine the basics of strikes, blocks, and grappling. And honestly, the combination of your mother's body and mine gave you a body that was perfectly balanced in speed, strength, and agility. There is so much raw potential in you, and all it needs is someone who can see how to bring it out."

"Father, can we never discuss your body and Mother's combining *ever again*?" Lunen asked with a disgusted look.

"Ah…sorry, son." Kabern smiled sheepishly. "The point is, I did study every combat art, and then I removed what didn't work for me. I'm going to help you develop advanced combat skills that you cannot only perform but combine. And then, I'll help you learn how to bring your moons together to create a style all your own."

Lunen clenched and unclenched his fists, trying to work up the nerve to ask his father something he thought he would never learn. "Father, why did you learn all these fighting styles?"

"Because, when I was a small boy, a dear friend of mine died saving me during a horrible sandstorm. When I faced his parents, I expected them to hate me, but they said that they could only hate me if I did not do anything to honor his sacrifice." Kabern took a deep breath. "I hoped to become a man who was as good a person he could have been, a man who would always be able to help those he cared about. So, I traveled the world so I could be strong enough to protect anything, and I made sure that I was able to live with myself after each choice. And when I died, I think I managed to die as the man I wanted to be."

Lunen smiled as he heard the story. He never got to hear stories from his father about his past before he died, and hearing it now helped Lunen understand why his father died saving him. His father chose to be the best of what he wanted to be, and he died still doing what he knew was the right thing.

"Thank you," Lunen said, hugging his father for the first time in more than a decade. "So, how should we start?"

"Well, which do you want to learn first, Southern Gold Whirling arms, or Western Red Cyclone kicks? After we do some work in agility-based arts, we'll move on to raw power arts and then speed. Finally, we'll combine what you learned physically with what you can imagine using your Blue-moon with, and by then... you'll either be dead, or someone I wouldn't want to fight," Kabern said, smiling a very familiar smile. For once Lunen understood how Winnie felt when he smiled before a training session, and he silently promised not to smile like that again if this was the effect it had.

Winnie swung her staff around slowly, going through the motions as she looked at the red light of the moon shining on the crystals lining the ceiling. *Almost makes me wonder what the Blue moon looks like,* she thought.

"You're a strange one," Ellamar said as she wiped the sweat from her brow. After finally mixing the pieces of the dagger with the blood in the molten metal, she removed the metal and journeyed to another room that had a wide window, an anvil, and a furnace. She had then spent the time since sunset with hammer and tongs, shaping and bending the glowing metal. As she did that, Winnie starting going through her attacks, but it seemed to the Blood-Forger as if she was overextending her reach. "How far away is the opponent in your mind?"

"Izoln's sword has as much reach as my staff," Winnie said, pivoting on her heel while whirling the staff around. "If I'm going to be able to slow him down, I need to close that distance."

"I bet your Blood-Steel would make something interesting." Ellamar chuckled as she began hammering again.

"How does Blood-Steel work, anyway?" Winnie asked, practicing a motion that in theory could raise a blocking sword and strike an opponent's abdomen in the next moment. "I mean, is it a special metal, like the gaianite or gelix the airship uses? Or is it something more mystic than that?"

"Ah, the questions of the young," Ellamar said, taking the huge piece of metal and shoving it again into the nearby furnace. "Have you ever heard of the power of positive thinking? That it can be the difference between success and failure?"

"Isn't that just another thing about being confident?" Winnie asked.

"Yes, but it's also a statement about the energy we put out in the universe," Ellamar said, her voice taking a more serious tone than Winnie had ever heard from her. She pulled the metal from the furnace and placed it back on the anvil. "Every hope, every action, puts out energy, which subtly changes the chance of success or failure. Energy never truly vanishes. Blood is a conduit for life energy. A Blood-Forger, after spending years reading blood and practicing on making pots and cutlery, should be able to let the energy in their body communicate with the raw energy in the blood. We call it out, allow it take hold of the metal, and change it as the blood must, while it tells us what shape to make it."

"So, the blood is what makes the strange powers in the metal?" Winnie asked, stepping closer to peer at the glowing lump being shaped.

"Yes, and usually the shape and power of the Blood-Steel becomes an expression of the warrior who uses it. Sometimes it shapes itself into a weapon the user is already well versed in; other times, it shapes itself to something the warrior has never seen before. Izoln's sword is an expression of his drive, and his anger. He wishes to reach his goal and obliterate it completely. That is what determined its shape and its ability."

"So, what would Lunen's be?" Winnie asked, trying hard not to also ask what she thought her own blood would make.

"Judging from what the blood is telling me, Lunen seeks no change in the kind of person he is, only a chance to show what he is truly capable of."

In the realm of the spiritual arena, Lunen's father trained him to his limits and then beyond. And, as they were not in the physical realm, they had no reason to sleep or eat. Their injuries would vanish as they paused from the training, and then they continued, spending the second day of the trance in sparring.

Kabern was not concerned with making his son a master of any individual form. Instead, he focused on making Lunen a master of individual techniques. As Lunen continued from one move to the next, he was already starting to imagine how to combine them. His father, a true genius of fighting, saw that Lunen's greatest strength was being able to surprise his opponents. Now, he had skill to match his heart.

"Why aren't you teaching me weapon arts?" Lunen asked as his father sparred with him. The Triblood kept twisting at the hips as he spun on his feet, his extending and already turning arms becoming a tornado of movement as he deflected several punches.

"Why? You expecting you'll need them?" Kabern asked, dropping backward on his hands while kicking his son's feet out from under him.

Before, Lunen would have simply fallen. Now, his arms braced his landing as he fell forward. Using their strength, he managed to spin his body on his palms, bringing both his feet at his father. His father flipped backward, getting back on his feet and launching a low roundhouse kick. Lunen relaxed his arms, dropping onto his back. The kick sailed over him, and he quickly flipped back onto his feet. The two both threw straight punches with their right hands, connecting at the wrist. Lunen twisted his hand around, grabbing his father's arm and pulling it down. As his left hand shot forward, Kabern punched out with his left to counter.

Lunen opened his palm, grabbing Kabern's left wrist and pulling it down while simultaneously releasing his right hand's grip. The Triblood then brought his right fist over the now-tangled limbs of his father and struck with all his strength on his father's chest. As the older man flew backward, Lunen pursued. Kabern rolled backward as he landed. As he stopped in a crouch, his son launched into a double-kick, his left foot forcing his father to open up a little in order to block, leaving his chest wide open for Lunen's right. Kabern lay on his back again, with his son's knee pressed on his chest.

"Father, how will I know how to use my new weapon if you don't teach me?"

"Son, there are no secrets from the dead. When the trance is over, you'll be ready to use it."

Then they began sparring again for yet another day.

Izoln smiled as he crawled. After a week of walking, he had finally caught up to the *Freewind*. They thought that by keeping the ship right at the top of the Blood-Forgers' stairway, they would see him coming. But he had spent a lifetime learning not only to fight but to study, track, and sneak. He had already coated his body with one of the strongest perfumes he could find, since he already knew that the Triblood had a pet sky-lynx. He was not in the mood to kill any that were not his target when it was possible to just pass by them.

He commended himself for his plan. After all, they could not imagine he would try an infiltration from the very corner of the canyon. As he finally shifted to his feet and began a quick dash, Izoln leapt toward one of the many openings that allowed light into the Blood-Forgers' city. He narrowly managed to grip the edge and could feel his hand sweat as the steam drifted out. But when he pulled himself, he quickly charged forward, feeling his cloak lift and move with both his actions and the hot, humid air.

Once he cleared the opening, he leapt down to a distant rooftop, rolling with the impact. The Fight-Hunter then began to leap from roof to roof, the Temple his single focus. He had already reasoned that the Triblood would probably seek out a replacement weapon, and he knew from experience the anticipation that would root a man to the Temple until the weapon was finished. With luck, Izoln would be able to kill Lunen before it was completed.

He shifted his speed, slowly walking through the Temple in search of his prey. He was shocked to find the Triblood lying on the ground, his eyes an eerie blue. He saw a small, wrapped bundle next to his target and remembered how the Blood-Forgers refused to let anyone besides the one who forged the weapon see what it was before its master could.

"I can't believe it," Izoln said aloud, even when he knew Lunen was beyond hearing him. "They put you in a spirit trance? Even I didn't get a spirit trance." He began to approach his opponent, eyeing the bundle. "Well, your weapon doesn't look that impressive, but I'm not willing to take any chances." He reached for his sword.

"Well, that's interesting," Winnie said as she leaned against the wall by the opening, smiling at how Izoln focused so much on Lunen that he had failed to check the rest of the room for any sort of guard. "All this time, I kept hearing about how you always liked to fight fair, prove that you were stronger. And here you are, about to kill someone who can't fight back." She took a stance and brought her staff into position. "Guess you're just another gutless thug."

"Girl," Izoln said over his shoulder, not even bothering to face her, "the Triblood already lost to me, utterly. I'm only here to carry the fight to its logical conclusion, and repay him for my arm."

"Please," Winnie said. "If you didn't distract him by breaking his father's dagger, he would have finished you then."

"Your faith in him is intriguing," Izoln replied admiringly as he began wrapping the chain around his forearm. "If you want to challenge me for him, I'll accept, but don't expect mercy."

You don't have to win, Winnie thought. *Just keep him busy until Lunen wakes up. God, I hope that's soon.*

Izoln turned on the ball of his foot and charged, stabbing straight at Winnie with his long sword. Winnie became a blur as she dodged to the side, and as the wall exploded, the Fight-Hunter was shocked as thura bone crashed into the back of his head. He dived forward, going with the impact. As he went through the hole, he landed on his belly and rolled to the side, narrowly avoiding the strike from Winnie as she leapt after him. He rose quickly, swinging his sword in a wide arc. Winnie ducked, feeling a few strands of her auburn hair sever as she delivered a straight strike to Izoln's solar plexus.

As he backed up, Izoln began to realize that, for her lack of moons, Winnie was an exceptional staff fighter. She continued to impress him as she began a rapid series of circling strikes, forcing him to shield himself with his sword. He quickly thrust his left hand forward, grabbing her by the throat. As she gasped for air, he threw her out a nearby window with considerable strength. He leapt out after her and performed a double-kick to her stomach.

She felt the wind leave her as Izoln grabbed her by her shirt and landed in a crouch, holding her above him. Even holding back, he was still more than a challenge for her. He then dropped her to the ground, and began to walk back up the stairway to the Temple.

"We're…not done yet," Winnie panted, rising to her feet. She brought her staff back up to a ready position.

Izoln quickly turned and charged and, with a single swing, split the thura-bone staff in two. He smirked and began to walk away, convinced he'd proved his superiority. He was stunned to feel what he was sure were two halves of a staff hit him in the back. He turned to stare incredulously at her.

"You want to get near him," Winnie said, trying not to stumble from the repeated blows, "you're going to have to kill me first!"

"So be it!" Izoln yelled, leaping into the air, his sword raised high.

Please, let me have bought enough time! Winnie closed her eyes, wondering what the feeling of a split skull would be like before she died. Despite her lack of experience in the subject, she was sure it sounded nothing like a metallic *clang*. She opened her eyes and realized how used to this new life of hers she was when all she could do was smile.

Lunen stood shirtless, hunched down, his arms, now sheathed in simple-looking, centimeter-thick, black metal gauntlets that shielded his entire forearms and fists, crossed over his head—a perfect stance for absorbing the impact of the massive sword. His voice rose to a roar as he threw his arms wide open, forcing the already shocked Izoln to backpedal and take the sight in. He stood to his full height, and as he brought his right hand down dramatically to point at the Fight-Hunter, Winnie heard his mother's pendant seem to ring as it slid along its chain.

"It's one thing to try and kill me, but when you try to kill an unarmed girl who happens to be *my* friend, you've earned yourself a war you won't forget!" Lunen yelled as the Blood-Forgers and the *Freewind* crew finally began to finally arrive and see that a fight was about to begin.

In all the time I knew him, I saw Lunen as several things, both good and bad. He was childish, funny, temperamental, understanding, and violent. But above all, I knew he was a good man. And seeing him just show up, seemingly different from the way I knew him, almost older somehow but still the same good man, it felt as if I was watching something evolve into a greater stage. And for the first time, I looked forward to seeing him beat the living daylights out of someone.

CHAPTER 8: Rebirth

Lunen rubbed his arms as he sat on the arena floor. His father was dusting his cloak off, trying not to show any sign that training his son was actually wearing him down.

"It's strange," Lunen grunted. "I feel like my muscles are tensed, like coiled springs."

"Shouldn't be such a surprise," Kabern said. "After all, while you've been in the trance, your muscles in the world of flesh have been constantly twitching, committing to their memory the skills you've learned here."

Lunen stood and slowly turned, taking in the arena. He noticed that the walls were starting to dissolve. "The trance is ending, isn't it?" he asked, feeling a lump in his throat.

"Sadly, yes." Kabern stood next to his son and placed a hand on his shoulder.

"Father…I always wanted to ask," Lunen said, trying not to let the tears he felt rising show, "why did you and Mother flee north? Why guarantee that I would be born a Triblood?"

"It was your mother's decision," Kabern replied as the dissolution of the blue world continued down the arena seats toward them. "I told her I was afraid that if you were born a Triblood, the world would forever be against you. But the truth was, I was afraid that *I* wouldn't accept you if you were born that way."

The dissolution closed in around them, and the dust of the floor began to scatter to the ether.

"She told me that north would be more hospitable than south, thanks to the Blue-mooners and the way they shifted nature, and that the differences that had our homes at odds back then would keep us from being safe anywhere else. She also said that, in the end, birth means nothing. Only what is done with life."

There was nothing left in the blue world now but the two of them.

"It's time, son," Kabern said quietly.

"It wasn't fair," Lunen said. "Both of you dying for such stupid reasons. It just wasn't fair."

"It wasn't," the larger man replied, turning to face his son, "but you've done so well in spite of it. We're both proud of you. You could have easily broken, fallen to what they thought of you. Instead, you kept going. Now, you're ready to be the man you know in your heart is the best you can be."

"And what kind of man is that?" Lunen asked, his voice cracking slightly.

"A man who can pursue what he wants and still stay true to what he knows in his heart is right. You've always tried to understand the lessons life gave you, every time you spoke of them to that girl. Now, you're ready to truly live them."

"You know about Winnie?" Lunen asked, worried about what that meant.

"Yes. Your mother and I approve, by the way," Kabern added with a smirk.

"F-father!" Lunen stammered. "It's not like that!"

"Of course it isn't," Kabern said, giving his son a playful wink as his feet began to dissolve away.

"No, not yet!" Lunen cried, tears falling freely now. "There's so much I want to ask!"

"You're ready," Kabern said. "There is a darkness watching you, Lunen, and I cannot be there when you face it. But I will watch, and I know you'll make us proud."

"Father!" Lunen tried to grab his father, to hug him, to tell him that he always loved him. But the larger man was gone.

"I love you," he said quietly.

"Of course you do," the voice of Kabern said from a seemingly great distance, "I'm the greatest father in the world!" A maniacal laughter followed it, and Lunen smiled despite himself.

Lunen blinked his eyes, hoping he had not cried in the real world. After all, he had a reputation to maintain. He felt disgusting after lying down in a sweltering forge for three days, and he pulled his drenched shirt from his torso as he stood. Lunen saw the bundle and felt drawn to it.

He heard the sound of metal against what he began to recognize as thura bone and turned to see a large, perfectly circular hole in the wall. The last time he saw anything that large and round, it was a crater after dodging a stab from Piercing Resonance. He tore the cloth from his weapon, and when his flesh touched the metal gauntlets, he knew their name and what they could do. His father not teaching him weapons made sense finally.

He ran through the hole, following the sounds of battle as he fastened both gauntlets to his arms. He quickly made his way outside to the top of the massive stairs of the Temple.

"You want to get near him," he heard Winnie's voice cry. He found her at the bottom of the stairs, struggling to remain standing as she faced Izoln, his back to the Triblood. "You're going to have to kill me first!"

Lunen began running down the stairs, willing the air to shift around him so that his already-great speed would increase. He knew that most men like Izoln would probably take her up on the offer, especially if she was the one who had fought the Fight-Hunter from the room he was in during his trance all the way out here.

"So be it!"

Lunen slid under the Fight-Hunter as he leapt, twisting on his feet to face him. He enjoyed Izoln's shocked face as he crossed his arms and widened his legs, bracing for the impact. He was thankful for the new gauntlets. Not only would they be able to absorb the sword's blow, but he would be able to make it look impressive when it happened.

A metallic *clang* rang out, and Lunen felt his muscles, like coiled beasts, spring up as he threw his arms open with a roar. In one swift motion, he brought his right hand down to point at Izoln.

"It's one thing to try and kill me, but when you try to kill an unarmed girl who happens to be *my* friend, you've earned yourself a war you won't forget!"

He heard his blood pounding in his ears and felt his breath flowing in and out of him. He could not deny it: the chance to settle the fight with Izoln excited him, the chance to use what he had learned, to show the world just what kind of man he truly was. And his chance was coming, for the Blood-Forgers and his crew had arrived.

"I don't know how you got past us," Liana said, drawing her swords, "but you're insane if you think you're getting out of this alive." Wind-hunter growled at her side, and the others, from Lei-to to Zeg, drew their weapons as well.

"Sorry, Captain," Lunen said as he started to bounce on the balls of his feet, "but he's mine."

"Lunen, this isn't up for discussion."

"I thought I was like a brother to you!"

"Don't let some crazy old woman put ideas in your head…no offense."

"None taken," Ellamar said as she broke from the crowd, walking slowly to a position between the Triblood and the Fight-Hunter. "However, I cannot let anyone interfere in this fight."

"Thank you," Lunen said with a bowed head amidst loud protests from the crew.

"It is the custom in our home," Ellamar said, loud enough for all to hear, "that if two of our Blood-Steel weapons are about to clash, we will not interfere in the fight." She then walked over to Winnie, who was still amazed that she could stand after the beating she'd taken.

"Do I want to know why?" Winnie asked the priestess.

"Honestly, we get out of this city so rarely that we never get to see the fruits of our labors," Ellamar replied, the laughter shining in her eyes.

Lunen smiled and then turned to face Izoln. He brought both his fists together and bowed. Izoln's smile was empty as he brought his sword over his head and down again to point it at the Triblood.

"Are you sure you want to try this again?" Izoln asked. "After all, you had a real weapon last time, and you still lost."

"It's not the blood or the weapon," Lunen said as he brought his open left hand out and pulled his closed right one to his waist, "it's the man."

"The man seemed to be what lost last time."

"For the last time, I didn't lose. I got discouraged!" With that, Lunen closed the distance between them, right fist pulled back. Izoln grinned and swung his sword at the Triblood's neck. Lunen suddenly shifted in midstep, his arms extending in a wide, upward arc as he pivoted. The gauntlets collided with the flat side of the sword, lifting the blade over Lunen's head. Once the sword passed, he dropped low, using the momentum to add force to his sweeping legs.

Izoln quickly backpedaled and was shocked when Lunen suddenly sprang into a small backflip onto his hands, allowing the momentum to continue as his feet finally collided with the Fight-Hunter's head. Izoln stumbled as Lunen landed on his feet. He turned and took a long step to Izoln, his metal-encased right fist finally reaching the target's chest with brutal force. As Izoln was thrown backwards, he swung his sword again. Lunen leapt back, resulting in a huge gash across his bare chest, as opposed to a sword severing him in two. Izoln smashed into the stairs while Lunen fell onto the ground.

"Ow. I've got to give you credit; you're tenacious," Lunen breathed. "I mean, attacking while taking a hit; that's good."

"You're one to talk," Izoln grunted as he slowly stood up from the stairs, dusting chunks of rock from his cloak. "You combined moves from three different fighting styles. And since you didn't use them before, I can only guess you didn't know them then. So, you had to have learned enough in a week to be able to combine them so fluidly in a fight."

"No, I didn't," Lunen said, his voice taking on the familiar jocular tone his crewmates knew him for. "I only had three days to learn them."

Izoln stared, his face a mask of shock, before fading into rage as he charged forward, his sword pulled back. Lunen smiled, and as the sword stabbed toward his chest, he leapt, his tucked knees barely missing the blade's tip. He then extended his legs down, his boots slamming into the sword and angling it into the stone floor.

Lunen's smirk faded when he saw Izoln smile. The Fight-Hunter's left fist smashed into the Triblood's ribs, and he felt one break as he sailed backward into a stone house.

"You're not the only one who likes a good fist fight!" Izoln yelled triumphantly. A sudden distortion of air flew with blinding speed, crashing into Izoln's chest, leaving the indentation of a fist. Not only was he sent back to the stairs with incredible force, he actually bounced up them to the top, landing at the Temple's wide doorway.

"Maybe not," Lunen yelled from the ruined home he had crashed into, his fist still extended, "but I'm definitely more creative about it!" He then leapt forward, willing the air to again get out of his way, causing a burst of speed as he flew up the stairway. Izoln had barely stood before Lunen slammed into him, locking his arms around his opponent's waist. The two crashed through another wall into the blazing heat of the Temple's main forge.

Blood-Forgers scattered and evacuated as the two combatants quickly separated and rose to their feet. Lunen quickly rushed forward, his fist pulled back for another punch. Izoln smiled at his foe's seemingly repetitive tactics and swung horizontally toward the Triblood's neck. Lunen suddenly dropped onto his back, his legs kicking out and knocking Izoln upward. Lunen followed up with a strong blast of wind, propelling his opponent toward one of the suspended vats of molten metal. The Fight-Hunter twisted in the air, his sword severing one of the vat's supports.

"Oh, come on!" Lunen yelled as a stream of glowing, liquid metal rained down toward him. He flipped back up onto his feet and fired a constant burst of air straight up and held his breath, afraid that he would end up losing the air in his body as he felt the hairs on his flesh being pulled up by the vacuum. The liquid steel began to flow around the wind like milk flowing over a stone. They heard an audible hiss as the steel cooled, going from a glowing orange to a dull grey. He smiled as he thought about how before, he would have just dodged because he *never* would have believed that he could cool steel that quickly. His smile vanished, however, when he realized that his impressive trick had resulted in creating a blob-like cage around himself.

"Well…shit," Lunen sighed.

"Are you really this stupid?" Izoln asked disbelievingly as he landed.

"Oh, come on. I've never fought around molten metal!" Lunen yelled at his opponent. "How was I supposed to know it'd do that?"

"I was right," Izoln commented as he wrapped the chain of his sword around his forearm. "Killing you will be a service to the world."

As Izoln pulled his arm back for his trademark move, Lunen suddenly brought both his armored fists down onto the ground as hard as he could, cracking the stone floor beneath the cooled steel. And as the Fight-Hunter charged forward, the Triblood gripped the thick steel bar that stood between them, lifting the cage above his head before swinging it down in time to block the attack. The metal exploded, and the force sent Lunen flying. He came to a stop in front of a metal cauldron and sensed boiling water inside it. The Blood-Forgers must have used it to cool the metal after they finished their work. He felt inspiration.

"You really keep surprising me," Izoln said, walking slowly toward him. "Honestly, I heard that your talent for improvisation was your strongest skill."

"You don't know the half of it," Lunen commented with a smirk as he focused his will on the boiling water. The water began to swirl and churn and slowly rose into the air. Lunen thrust his open palm at Izoln, and the water threw itself at him. Izoln leapt straight up, but Lunen focused again, turning the water upward. Izoln howled in pain as he felt his legs burn. Lunen stood quickly and plunged his fists into the water, focusing for it to cool. As it did, he felt the water solidify around his gauntlets. He lifted the frozen water over his head and brought it down with great force. As it shattered, he concentrated on a shape, and when he rose up, a foot-long blade of ice clung to each gauntlet.

He turned and charged toward the falling Izoln, leapt forward, and was shocked as one foot slammed into his jaw, and another slammed into his crossed blades, smashing through them. Izoln had landed with his sword planted into the ground and swung his burnt legs around like clubs at the Triblood during his attack. Lunen stumbled but then lashed out with a reverse-roundhouse kick. Izoln soared through the air, rolling as he landed. He finally came to a stop next to a row of still-heating blades.

"Let me guess," Izoln panted. "This is all payback for what happened in our last fight?"

"We're way past notions of vengeance," Lunen grunted, his tongue pressing against his teeth in the hope that they were not loose. "You hunt warriors for some twisted sense of proving your worth to be alive, all because you have nothing else since getting your revenge on your father."

"Shut up!" Izoln screamed. "I fight to prove my strength! My life taught me that only the strong are allowed to live!"

"So, are you saying that your mother was weak because she died?" Lunen asked quietly as his fingers began to tighten into fists, "Or that you don't deserve to live because you couldn't protect her?"

"Shut up; shut up; shut up!" Izoln screamed, his heart was pounding as the adrenaline flowed through him. His legs were healing faster, and he began to stand to his full height.

"The strong exist to protect the weak!" Lunen yelled, his voice becoming firmer as his eyes began to burn into Izoln. "Those who fail to realize that shall learn how weak they really are."

"I'll kill you!" Izoln roared, grabbing one of the glowing blades and charging toward the Triblood as Lunen also began closing the distance between them.

Izoln swung wide, the burning blade cutting into Lunen's ribs as the Triblood's fist, using his Blue-moon to create a single point of vacuum, tore a gash in the Fight-Hunter's shoulder. They both came to a stop and glared at each other. Lunen began to think as his wound cauterized. The plan in his head had formed when the blade cut into his flesh, and yet it seemed entirely plausible. He opened his fingers as straight as he could and held his hands in front of him, his chest completely open. For the final touch, he smiled.

Izoln charged again, the smile setting him off. Lunen had learned in the arena that it was easy to anger an opponent by taking them less seriously. His hopes rested now on whether he was right about his strength, the gauntlets, and hot metal.

The glowing blade swung hard, and Lunen's right arm chopped at it. A loud metallic *clang* rang through the forge. Izoln swung again, and Lunen's left arm repeated the motion. The blade began swinging furiously, and their arms began to move and weave over and around each other. Lunen then stepped forward and slammed both his open palms into Izoln's chest, knocking him off balance. The Triblood then began attacking the glowing sword with as many points of his arm as possible, from the ridge of his palm to the gauntlets' cutoff point just before the elbow, in as many places on both sides of the sword as he could. He then finished with a single punch straight to the middle of the blade and stepped back.

Izoln took a moment to realize what had happened, and as he looked at the bent and twisted metal object in his hand, he just stared at Lunen in annoyance. "You're either insane or lucky," he said, tossing the weapon to the ground and slowly walking to his Blood-Steel sword.

"I really didn't think about that until you burned me," Lunen said, walking alongside him. "Seriously, I was making that up as I went."

"Interesting," Izoln replied, his tone indicating how contrary his feelings on the topic really were. "You know, traditionally, I don't do this. I consider it unfair on my opponents, assuming they aren't good enough."

"Ooooooh, now I'm curious," Lunen said, grinning, his own feelings now contrary to the tone he used.

"Not only are you proving hard to kill," Izoln growled, "but you're just pissing me off enough to justify it." With that, he tore his cloak off and threw it at Lunen.

Lunen's plan was to snatch the cloak in midair, pivot around, and toss it back as Izoln attacked him with Piercing Resonance. When his hand touched the cloak, he realized that would be impossible. The cloak was ridiculously heavy, and it landed in such a manner as to cover his upper torso. It also felt as if something hard was sown into the edges of the cape. Rather than act with his typical flair, Lunen let his body drop. He heard metal slice through the air above him, and as he rolled free, he saw Izoln had passed by him, his arm in the finishing motions of an outward slash.

"Nice cape," Lunen said, standing back up. "I'm going out on a limb here, but I'd say the fabric is denser that most, and it's also densely woven together. But the added weight in the edges…"

"Special ceramic plates," Izoln said, his irritation showing more and more as he turned to face Lunen. "It weighs me down, both exercising my muscles and giving my enemies a chance."

"I heard about a sect of warriors in the Twisted Jungle who used that training method," Lunen commented, kicking the remnants of the cape off him.

"A nice side effect of it all," Izoln said, a predatory smile returning to his lips, "is that taking it off makes me a lot faster."

Lunen learned that fact as Izoln blurred and finally reappeared behind him. He barely managed to turn and block with his gauntlets as the sword stopped just short of splitting his skull. A trickle of blood dripped slowly down the center of his forehead as he clenched his teeth and began to push back. Izoln sidestepped and swung, and the Triblood felt his belly tear. The wound was not deep, but it bled enough for him to worry about binding it.

"What, no snappy remark?" Izoln commented, his grin widening. "No clever tactics?"

"Anyone ever tell you your sword is a huge sign of overcompensation?" Lunen offered, his fingers squeezing the flesh around his wound in hope of stifling the bleeding.

"Oh yes, my sword," Izoln seemed to sing as he began to wrap the chain around his forearm. "Do you understand how my Piercing Resonance works?"

"I only figured it out after my spirit trance," Lunen said, taking a few steps back toward the burning coals. "The chain provides a link between your physical, mental, and spiritual energy, then sends it into the blade. It then vibrates at high frequencies, and when you stab something with it, the energy built in the sword releases straight forward and explodes anything in its path."

"Only half right," Izoln said as his forearm began to bulge. "You see, it's not limited to stabbing."

He lunged forward, slashing diagonally as Lunen leapt to the side. The blade slashed straight through the coal pit with an impossibly clean cut as the high frequency blade split the metal trough perfectly. Lunen reached up into the air, caught one of the flying coals, and slammed it against his belly wound. He screamed as it burned, and when he crashed onto his back on the stone floor, his abdomen was a scarred, smoking mess.

"Oooooh, clever, clever," Izoln said as he stalked toward him before delivering a kick strong enough to launch the Triblood again. "You know how Gold-mooners can heal faster with burns than cuts. Cauterize the wound, and your natural healing will take care of it. Of course, that's meaningless if you keep getting injured."

Lunen coughed up blood as he landed. He was sure he was bleeding internally, and while internal injuries healed faster, that did not help if he couldn't keep Izoln from attacking.

"It's strange," Izoln commented as he wrapped the chain around his arm again. "Usually there's some special trick to the Blood-Steel weapons, but yours seems exclusively for defense. Just makes me wonder if you're as cowardly as your weapon."

Lunen began to stand, despite the pain and dehydration. He brought his hands up to a ready position.

"Oh, this should be fun," Izoln said as he charged forward.

Winnie, Ellamar, and the rest had finally entered the main forge, just as Izoln closed the distance to his enemy. Lunen swung his right arm, a strange distortion circling the gauntlet before it collided with the side of the sword. A loud *bang* rang out as the impact forced the air from the combatants. Lunen continued with his momentum, shifting on his feet to bring his elbow straight into Izoln's face. As the Fight-Hunter rolled with the blow, the *Freewind* crew gave a hearty cheer.

"Your sword tells me a lot about you," Lunen coughed, wiping blood from his lips with his left hand as his right arm continued to swirl with what the observers now realized was wind around it. "You charge straight at whatever you want, no thought of what happens when or if you succeed. Kind of like this obsession you have with being strong." He brought his right arm back up to a ready position. "You keep going on about my limits. My gauntlets don't have some flashy attack trick, true. All they do is absorb anything that could damage my arms. But they let me strike with my full strength without worrying about breaking my fists. They let me focus and concentrate my elemental powers in ways that no Bluemooner could because of the damage their flesh could sustain. In other words, these Twin Guardians of mine let me go beyond my limits."

Lunen leapt into the air throwing a punch at Izoln, the cyclone blasting off his arm and smashing into the floor as Izoln dived past. The Fight-Hunter gave chase to the air, bringing his sword down at the Triblood as soon as he was in range. Lunen's gauntlets began to crackle and then glow as he focused lightning through the metal. When Piercing Resonance connected with Twin Guardians, it bounced back with full force as the current flowed through the metal and into its owner. Izoln forced himself to ignore the pain as his left hand grabbed Lunen's foot. When they landed, he brought the Triblood headfirst into the floor and then flung him over his shoulder to the far wall.

Lunen's head throbbed, and he saw the trail his blood was leaving in the sky as it flowed from the new gash on his forehead. He twisted in midair, landing with his feet against the wall. Izoln was already in the air, closing the distance between them at incredible speed, the chain once more wrapped around his forearm. The Triblood kicked off the wall toward the floor beneath his opponent and brought both his fists down with full force, focusing his will into the stone as they collided. A solid piece of stone shot straight up at Izoln, who brought his sword down and sliced cleanly through it.

His face, a picture of self-satisfaction, turned to shock as he saw Lunen beneath the stone, his fists ignited in flame as he leapt straight up. He brought his sword to a defensive position, hoping to deflect some of the blows. Rather than the expected rapid strike, Lunen slammed both fists into Izoln's chest, the flames exploding upon impact. The Fight-Hunter was launched straight up, smashing into the ceiling. He fell like a rag doll, and Lunen half-hoped that this meant the fight was over. At the last moment before he landed, Izoln flipped over onto his feet and thrust his blade straight through Lunen's abdomen. Six feet of steel passed through Lunen's body and out his back, stopping only because of the hilt.

The forge was silent. Shock settled over the crowd. Winnie nearly charged at Izoln, but Ellamar's hand on her own kept her still.

"People like us," Izoln said quietly as Lunen continued gasping, "people who live when others die, have to prove that we deserve our life. If we don't, then we die. It's that simple."

His muscles finally relaxed, and he began to draw the blade out. Suddenly Lunen's left hand clasped down on Izoln's right, pinning it to the hilt, keeping the blade from moving. The Triblood brought his right fist into Izoln's face.

"People like us..." Lunen growled. His fist swung back, the armored knuckles scoring another blow against Izoln's face. "People who lived because others died saving them..." he continued, his voice growing louder. His left hand let go of Izoln's, but the Fight-Hunter's grip on the sword remained tight as he saw Lunen's fist prepare to strike again. "*Should make them proud of the lives they saved!*" Lunen roared as he struck with every bit of strength he had.

Izoln was thrown backward, dragging the sword out with him. As he crashed against an empty metal vat, Lunen collapsed to one knee.

"I don't know about you," Lunen said, struggling to stand as a ball of flame ignited over his open palm, "but I'm sick of letting my past control me."

To the shock of everyone, he slammed the fireball into his wound. As he screamed in agony, a burst of flame shot out from his back. The air smelled of seared meat. The Triblood stood to his full height, burn scars slowly healing on his abdomen and back.

"So you'd just forget it," Izoln growled as he used his sword to help himself to his feet, blood dripping from his nose and mouth. "Just ignore how others died because of how we were born?"

"I'll remember it," Lunen said before coughing up more blood, "but in the end, it's all about living in the present, so that I can make sure that I live my life with no regrets, like I'm sure they did." He glanced over at his crew and smiled, hoping his bloodied teeth were not too ghastly a sight.

Izoln smiled and then began to laugh. Lunen chuckled and began to laugh too. The crowd looked at both of these men silently, afraid of where the fight was about to go.

"You know, Lunen," Izoln said as he began to wrap his chain around his arm, "I still owe you for a broken arm."

"Likewise," Lunen replied, "but I'm afraid I only have strength left for one last hit."

"Same with me." Izoln smiled as he brought his sword to its ready position. "All or nothing?"

"Why not?" Lunen agreed.

Izoln took off at full speed, the ground cracking as he kicked off, and Lunen did the same. The Fight-Hunter put all his remaining strength into the attack. Lunen's right arm ignited in flame that swirled around his fist as he swung it. The Triblood's body began to wrap in flame, becoming a spiraling mass of fire, the right fist at the center point as it flew toward its target. Izoln thrust his sword straight at the center of the blazing tornado, all of Piercing Resonance's force striking at once.

The spectators were thrown to the ground as the wind passed over them following the explosion. When they got back to their feet, they saw a crater in each of the far walls, each with an unconscious body resting in it.

"Excited?" Lunen asked as he limped down the hall, a hand on the wall the only thing keeping his battered and bandaged body up.

"Yeah," Winnie replied, her ribs the only thing still hurting from the fight a week prior. "I mean, it's like weapon fortunetelling. I just can't wait to see what mine does."

"Just don't be surprised," Lunen grunted as they entered the main forge.

The rest of the *Freewind* crew already stood there, trying to stay out of the way as the Blood-Forgers continued repairs to the damage done by the battle. After digging the two warriors out of the wreckage, the Blood-Forgers had begun to take care of them, in spite of the damage they had caused. When Winnie asked, Ellamar explained that her people held infinite hospitality to those who allowed them to see the results of their labors. Ellamar then told Winnie that she was so impressed with the girl's talent that she wanted to make a Blood-Steel weapon for her.

It was not a complete vacation, however. Despite all the damage he had done, they had to put up with Izoln. He was unapologetic toward Lunen and made no indication that anything the Triblood said or did changed his outlook. However, a bizarre incident involving him, Liana, and the bathing spring had taken place. Since then, the Fight-Hunter had gone out of his way to charm her. As a result, his injuries had not fully healed yet.

"So, any good beatings today?" Lunen asked as he took a place next to Liana.

"Lunen, seriously, why couldn't you have just killed him?" Liana growled.

"Honestly, he's just too fun to fight," Lunen chuckled as he looked over at Izoln, who was glaring at him due to his proximity to the captain.

Winnie stood before Ellamar as she held a long bundle, the glowing molten steel of the vats shining behind her. Winnie extended her hands, waiting for the moment Lunen had described.

"You are a very interesting child, Winnie Winters," Ellamar said. "You show much fear in regard to...well, everything." She paused as the girl's face flushed. "But you also show the courage to confront those fears."

Winnie wanted to disagree. The fact that she ran away from her problems still burned inside her. But the curiosity about what her weapon was, for the high priestess to say all that about it, made her hold her tongue.

"It is with great pleasure and honor that I present you with your weapon!" With those words, she tore the covering from the weapon, revealing a long, white staff.

"What is it with her and staffs?" Lunen asked. He then doubled over as an elbow from Liana struck his barely-healed ribs.

Winnie took the weapon in her hand, and, just as Lunen described it, she knew its name was Shining Reach, and as she twirled it, the staff began to extend longer and then shorten. Finally, it was barely the length of a pencil. She quickly pocketed the weapon.

The crew gave a cheer. Liana then noticed Izoln stalking over to Lunen.

"Triblood Lunen," he said. "I've given thought to your words. I'm not sure if it's what she'd want, but I think my mother would expect me to make reparations to the families of the ones I've killed."

"Um…okay…" Lunen swallowed, uncertain of where this was going.

"Once I finish, I will find you, and we'll settle it once and for all."

"Oh, come on!" Winnie exclaimed as she walked over to the crew. "He pretty much had you beat when the fight was over."

"Girl, don't think that a new weapon means you're a match for me," Izoln growled.

"Listen, Izoln," Liana said, "stay away from my crew, and maybe I'll reconsider my plans to have you killed one day."

"OK. For you, I'll spare the girl," Izoln replied with a predatory smile, "but the Triblood is mine."

"It's OK, Liana," Lunen said, cutting off whatever response the captain had for the Fight-Hunter. "I look forward to the next match."

"There is something I think you should know," Izoln said. "My dream was to be the world's greatest warrior. To prove that, I attempted an attack on the Masked Emperor while he was in a meeting about some tower. He beat me without even touching me. He said that if I wanted a rematch, he'd face me man to man—if I could beat the Triblood Lunen."

As he walked away, the *Freewind* crew attempted to process what they'd just heard. The Masked Emperor had once again attempted to kill Lunen specifically. More disturbing was the news that the tyrant was searching for the Tower as well.

"What should we do?" Winnie asked.

"I'm thinking; I'm thinking," Liana said quickly.

Lunen remained silent, but he already had a plan.

He moved between structures as the breaking sunlight bounced off the city's mirror system. Lunen traveled light, since his only possessions were his clothing and his gauntlets. He knew he would be lonely, but the Triblood understood a message when it was being sent.

"There is a darkness watching you, Lunen, and I cannot be there when you face it."

The Masked Emperor wanted him dead, and he knew that he would not stop unless he died—or the Emperor was dealt with. And Lunen knew that if he wanted to go after the most dangerous man in the world, he had to do it alone. He may have come to terms with his fears about letting others get hurt because of him, but he still felt he had to do what was necessary to protect them.

However, just as he came to the gates of the city, he heard the familiar sound air made when it was displaced at a great speed. He pivoted on the ball of his foot and brought his metal-sheathed arms into a cross-block. As the white metal pole slammed down, he sighed.

"You really thought you'd be able to sneak off on me?" Winnie asked as she willed her staff to shrink down. Wind-hunter stood by her legs, staring at his master as if being left behind hurt him.

"Winnie, you don't understand," he said as he straightened up. "If anything happened to you because of me…"

"Lunen," she said as she closed the distance between them. "If there's anything I've learned from you, it's that if you can help your friends, you should. You've helped me so much since I came here. It's time I helped you."

"Winnie," he said quietly, "why couldn't you learn to throw lightning? I mean, it'd be nice for someone else to do it."

They both grinned and began to walk out the gate. As they finished ascending the stairs, Wind-hunter walking between them, they passed by the *Freewind.*

"Where the hell do you three think *you're* going?" Liana's voice screamed from the deck.

Winnie and Lunen turned to see the entire crew assembled on the deck, staring down at them.

"Seriously, did everyone just wake up before me the one day I decided not to sleep in?" Lunen asked incredulously.

"Get up here!" the captain commanded.

After climbing the rope ladder to the deck, the two ended up staring down the core leaders of the crew.

"Listen, guys…" Lunen began as Wind-hunter finally landed on the deck.

"You made me a promise once, Lunen," Liana interrupted. "You said that you'd help support me and help me become as good a captain as my father."

"Her father was a good man," Leito added. "And when one member of the crew was in trouble, he did what he had to do to help them."

"Basically, if the Emperor wants ya, he's gotta deal wit' us first," Zeg added as he twirled a wrench on his fingers.

"Besides," Migs said as he patted Lunen on the shoulder, "you are such a good source of interesting injuries, I cannot just let you wander off and get hurt without being able to document it."

"Did I mention I hate my friends?" Lunen said to Winnie, a smile on his face.

"So, what's the plan, Captain?" Winnie asked, trying hard not to smile too much.

"Well, after careful thought, I decided to do something we may not all like," Liana said. "Since Izoln mentioned the Emperor's interest in the Tower…"

"Juushikahn?" Lunen asked, the disdain evident in his voice.

"He's not that bad," Winnie countered. "I mean, since the Tower seems to be the big thing in all this, he's the best chance we have of getting it before the Emperor does."

"You just want it so you can go home," Lunen retorted dejectedly.

"Well, yeah," she said, putting a hand on his shoulder. "But I'm not going until I repay you."

Lunen smiled and hugged her. As much as these people around him sometimes bothered him, he was happy for their presence in his life. And he had a feeling that things were about to get more interesting for them all.

Lunen seemed changed since his battle with Izoln. And with the threat of the Emperor, he seemed ready to stop simply living in the world and actually try to change it. We had no choice now but to help Juushikahn's resistance, find the Tower, and bring an end to the Masked Emperor's reign.

But the universe is funny, and when something happens, something will happen in reaction to the original action. And life on our ship was about to get very dangerous.

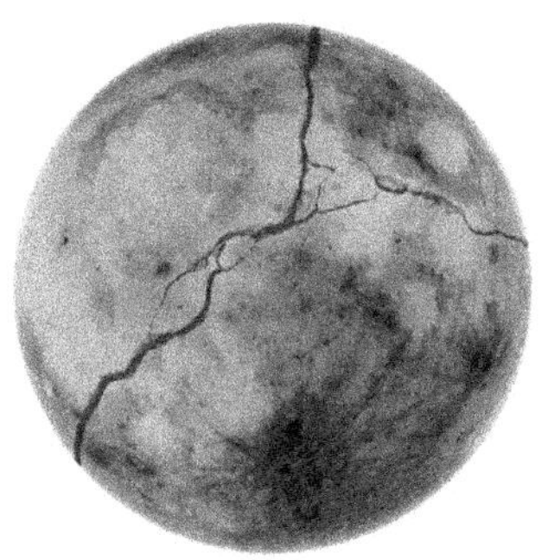

Epilogue

Beneath his armor, the soldier was shaking. He had seen and done many things in his life that would harden a man. He had aided General Imakur in the burning of a village whose inhabitants had decided that if they united in not paying taxes, they could send a message to other villages that the Empire could be stood up to. He had once knowingly escorted Disana, the Masked Emperor's sister, lover, and assassin, to the home of a noble in the Gold continent so she could kill his eight-year-old son as a message when said noble was plotting an insurrection. And since being reassigned to the Imperial Palace as a guard, he had more than once dragged a disrespectful servant to his master's throne room to be punished in a gruesome manner.

But these two terrified him beyond all reason. The elder one, a man in his thirties with ratty red hair that draped over his eyes, wore a shoddy suit with an equally ruined cloak. A thin mustache crowned his mouth. Next to him stood a young girl in a very bright pink, frilly dress, her blonde hair tied in a braid that reached well past her waist. While the man stood there with a smile devoid of mirth or kindness, she appeared too sullen in comparison. Her blue eyes stared into his through his helmet when she turned to face him—her blue, unblinking eyes.

The man was named Malagos, the child, Lensa, and he knew in his heart that if he gave them a reason to, they would kill him in a manner that would make what he had seen and done seem like nothing, because Malagos would genuinely enjoy the act alone. They were the Crimson Hunters.

When the Masked Emperor wanted to wage war on someone, he sent Imakur. When he wanted someone killed swiftly and subtly, he sent Disana. When he wanted a death so horrific and bloody that it would haunt one's nightmares into the afterlife, making a messy example of the horror he could send you, he sent the Crimson Hunters. As the soldier watched them enter through the opening doors to the throne room, he felt a great swell of pity for their next targets.

"So," Malagos asked, his voice seeming to somehow sing the words more than say them, "you want us to kill all the crew of the *Freewind*?"

"Exactly," the Masked Emperor said from his throne, Disana standing on his left and Imakur on his right.

"All of them?" Lensa asked, her high voice showing no enthusiasm for what was to happen. "No survivors?"

"Them, and anyone else who gets in your way," came the growling response, eliciting happy giggling from the grown man rather than the child.

The throne room fell silent for a few brief moments after the Crimson Hunters left. Then came a horrified scream, followed by the sound of armor being torn, then flesh doing the same. The screaming rose higher and higher until suddenly being cut off, followed by the sound of childish giggling that grew into a deep, maniacal laugh.

"I'm beginning to think I should include reflective visors for the guards," the Emperor said nonchalantly. "They never seem to understand the meaning of 'Do not look the Hunters in the eye.'"

"Which one?" his consort Disana inquired.

"Does it really matter which one?"

"Master, are you sure this is the right course?" Disana asked, the concern in her voice palpable. "Aren't you worried about the plan?"

"My dear sister," the masked man said, not even bothering to turn to her, "if my calculations are correct, Lunen knows I'm after the Tower. With my attempts on his life fueling not just his but his crew's actions, they'll seek it out. And that will be of great aid. If Malagos can kill him, then it just proves he wasn't the one I needed."

"My lord." Imakur turned to face his master, dropping to one knee. "Does it not concern you that Malagos seems intent on your death one day?"

"No," the Masked Emperor said, rising. "Everything I've learned suggests that Lunen and his friends have the skills necessary to bring my plan to fruition." He began to stalk away from the throne. "Results come faster with pressure. Malagos will help push them toward my goals, and, if worse comes to worst, they'll kill each other. Either one dies, it helps me in the end."

He turned to face them, pulling the mask from his face, the smile evident in his voice. "If he lives, then the Triblood is going to help me bring the conquest of this world to its conclusion." He brought his hand up as if he were holding something in his grip. "And when it is over, and he realizes what he's done, I'll tear Lunen's heart from his chest as his woman watches."

To Be Concluded in
Lunen
Book 2: Endgame

www.ingramcontent.com/pod-product-compliance
Lightning Source LLC
Chambersburg PA
CBHW070629310726
48982CB00001B/221
9780692795415